Sugar Daddy

A SUGAR BOWL NOVEL

SAWYER
BENNETT

LS

LOVESWEPT
NEW YORK

Sugar Daddy is a work of fiction.
Names, places, and incidents either
are products of the author's imagination
or are used fictitiously. Any resemblance
to actual events, locales, or persons,
living or dead, is entirely coincidental.

A Loveswept Trade Paperback

Published in the United States by Loveswept,
an imprint of Random House,
a division of Penguin Random House LLC, New York.

This book contains an excerpt from
the forthcoming book *Sugar Rush*
by Sawyer Bennett. This excerpt has been
set for this edition only and may not reflect
the final content of the forthcoming edition.

ISBN 978-0-399-17858-0
Ebook ISBN 9781101968123

Printed in the United States of America on acid-free paper

randomhousebooks.com

1 2 3 4 5 6 7 8 9

Book design by Elizabeth A. D. Eno

To Sue Grimshaw and Gina Wachtel. For believing in me.

To Lisa, Darlene, Janett, Karen, and Beth. Best beta readers in the whole damn world. I couldn't do this without you.

Sugar Daddy

PROLOGUE

Sela

"Come on. Up you go. Time to get you home."

A hand grips me at my upper arm and pulls me from the bed. My head spins and bile rises in my throat. I'm dizzy and hurt everywhere.

"Hey now," he chides me. "You forgot to button your jeans."

I look down through blurry eyes and watch in a daze as his hands work at my zipper, pulling it up and then fastening the button. I sway back and forth, my legs feeling like they're filled with Jell-O.

"There now. You're all presentable," he says with a dark laugh, and his hand is back on my arm. He guides me down a long hallway. I stumble twice, but he hauls me back up, his fingers digging into my flesh painfully. He leads me to a large, curved staircase and my right hand goes out to hold on to the wrought-iron banister. I stare in odd fascination at the dark ring of bruises around my wrist, which causes me to miss the first step and I almost go down.

"Easy now," he says in a gentle voice as he uses his grip on my arm to catch me. "Don't want you falling down these stairs and breaking your neck now, do we?"

A surge of fear wells up inside of me and I drop my eyes to my feet, watching as he carefully escorts me down the staircase. Blaring music, the chatter of maybe a hundred voices and people laughing.

Party noise.

My head is so heavy that it's a monumental effort to lift it when we reach the bottom, and my heels practically slide out from underneath me when they hit the slick marble tile of the grand foyer. I remember thinking it was so pretty when I first walked in.

"JT . . . man, she is a mess," someone says . . . a man. I recognize his voice. I call on every muscle in my neck to cooperate and raise my head, swiveling it to the left.

Ice-cold, pale blue eyes laugh at me. Thin blond hair so colorless it's almost white. Skin almost as ghostlike.

Albino?

He's smirking at me. A knowing look.

"Oh, fuck, she feels good," he moans as he slams in and out of me. I try to push him off me but I can't move my arms. I lift my head, first connecting my gaze with pale, evil blue eyes as they squint in grotesque pleasure, and then tilt my head backward. Someone . . . can't really see him . . . holding my wrists down.

I shake my head, trying to clear it of the horror.

"Let me dump her in a cab and then she won't be our mess anymore," the guy holding my arm says. I force my head to turn his way, my vision still going in and out of focus.

He's tall.

Really tall. Dark blond hair.

That's all I get.

My tongue feels so thick and I'm not sure my words come out right. "Who are you?"

"Baby," he says with what I think is a grin. A gray haze clouds my eyes and I see what I think are a row of sparkling teeth flashing at me. "I just made all your fantasies come true. Don't you remember?"

The guy with the pale eyes laughs hysterically, but I can't muster up the energy to look back at him. My head drops and I stare at the white and black diamond tiles and the tips of my red heels.

More pressure on my arm and I'm guided across the foyer. The music is so loud it hurts my ears and the laughter . . . is everyone laughing at me? Even though I'm not sure, I feel my cheeks burning with embarrassment.

"Allow me to get the door," a deep voice says, and I struggle to lift my gaze . . . narrow my eyelids to focus, and see someone reaching for a heavy, black iron door with a scroll design over frosted glass. On his wrist . . . that tattoo.

"Think she'll suck my dick?" Tan hands work at a belt buckle, slips the leather free, and pops the top button. A red bird on the inside of his wrist.

Pain shoots through my scalp as someone grabs my hair. I can feel a deep-seated scream start to push up from my throat, but it's so dry, it never makes it out.

"I don't know," a man says with a laugh from behind me, gives my head a shake. "She might bite it. I'd fuck her somewhere else if I were you. There's two other holes."

Pain . . . terrible, horrible pain in my ass . . .

I'm finally able to scream, but it's cut off as something is shoved in my mouth.

I think it's my panties.

The door swings open slowly and the faceless, blurry man

leads me through it. Three concrete steps down and my feet hit gravel. My ankles immediately roll from the uneven terrain and my knees start to buckle.

The man hauls me up again and then slips a supportive arm around my waist.

"You really are a mess," he says almost tenderly.

The cool night air helps to clear my mind a bit. I turn my head . . . easier now, and look at him again.

Brown eyes.

He has brown eyes.

How did I not notice that before?

He must sense that I'm looking at him, because he turns and tilts his head to look down at me. His eyes roam over my face and he gives an almost apologetic smile as he releases my arm to lift his hand. I close my eyes briefly as his fingertips come up to my hair just near my temple.

"Damn, baby . . . sorry . . . looks like we left some spunk in your hair," he says with a taunting laugh.

What?

My own hand raises and I touch my blond locks in confusion. There's something in my hair . . . stiff and brittle-feeling.

"I'm going to come," he grunts as he rams in and out of me so hard it feels like my hips are going to dislocate. "Hold her mouth open."

Something presses into the hinges of my jaw, forcing my mouth open. The cotton panties in my mouth are pulled out and I suck in air. The man on me . . . in me right now . . . blurred and shadowed.

Tears in my eyes making it even harder to see.

"That's it," he groans, slams into me one more time, then abruptly he's gone. I can hear a snapping sound, someone straddling my chest, and then warm, wet liquid starts dribbling into my mouth, hitting my cheek . . . my temple.

Laughter.

Men laughing.

I choke in surprise on the bitter taste, my tongue working to push it back out, but then a large hand is clamped over my mouth and nose, cutting off my air supply.

"Swallow it," he says gruffly. "All of it."

My throat contracts, releases, and then I swallow and choke. I blink the tears from my eyes as he rolls off me. I turn my head to the left and watch him pull his pants up. His chest is naked.

And there's a huge red bird tattooed across his ribs.

I jerk back from his touch and almost fall on my butt. He chuckles and wraps his arm around my waist tighter.

"Easy now," he says in a soothing tone, and starts to walk me down the gravel driveway to where a yellow car sits.

A cab.

"Where are you taking me?" I ask, my own voice sounding like a faraway echo.

"I'm taking you home. What's your address?"

I give it to him, hoping he can understand what I say, because I can't.

"You were great, baby. Want to do that again sometime, come back and ask for JT."

"I didn't like that," I insist in a thick voice. I'm starting to feel nauseous again. It hurts really bad between my legs . . . my butt . . .

"Doesn't matter," he says arrogantly. "You won't remember it tomorrow anyway."

The back door of the cab opens and I'm lowered into the seat. My head, which feels like it weighs five hundred pounds, falls back until it presses into the foam cushion. I can hear my address being given to the driver.

I close my eyes and surrender to the darkness.

• • •

"Come on, honey . . . wake up." A large hand shakes me by my shoulder. I peel my eyes open, my head now pounding. I push up from the cold vinyl seat and realize I'm in a car.

The backseat of a car.

"Get going." Pushing my hair out of my face, I see a portly Indian man staring at me with dark brown eyes. "I've got another fare to collect."

Swinging my legs out, I exit the backseat, realizing I don't have my purse. Did I even have it tonight?

"I don't have anything to pay you with," I mumble as I pat my back jeans pockets, vaguely remembering I had a large purse with me tonight but no clue where it is right now.

"Already taken care of," he says, and I wonder who paid him. I sort of remember someone helping me into the cab, but now I'm not sure.

I look over the top of the cab and see my house with the cheerful yellow light awaiting me on the front porch.

"Thank you," I mutter, and walk around the back of the cab. When I reach the mailbox at the end of my driveway, I hold on to it with one hand as I lean to the side and remove first one high heel, then the other. I leave them lying there. Oddly, my feet don't hurt, but that might be the only part of me that doesn't. I immediately feel steadier as my bare feet traverse the concrete driveway up to the small sidewalk that cuts across the front yard to the porch.

I make it up the four small steps and manage to reach on top of the doorframe for the spare key. The house is quiet when I walk in, both of my parents presumably sound asleep.

I try to be as quiet as I can as I walk down the short hallway, periodically reaching my hand out to steady myself on the wall. At my desk, I pull the chair out and sit down heavily, a pained cry coming out as another sharp stab of pain reverberates through my bottom. Tears well up in my eyes and I grab clumsily at my journal.

Opening the small spiral notebook, I don't bother trying to find the next available page. I just open it up somewhere around the middle and pick up my blue gel pen beside it. I write slowly, disregarding the drip of tears on the pages beside my words.

Today is my 16th birthday.

I was raped.

I think I deserved it.

The pen falls from my fingers as I push up from my desk. I close the notebook and stand from the chair, feeling beyond weary. My soul feels dank. My heart fragile like spun glass.

Red birds.

White hair.

Pain.

Spunk in my hair.

I walk back out of my room, down the hallway and through the living room. Into the darkened kitchen where I don't even bother turning on a light. What I need is in the utility drawer right by the entrance, and there's enough moonlight coming in through the windows over the sink so I can see well enough.

It takes but a moment to pull the drawer open and for me to grab it with surety.

Back down the hall and into the bathroom.

I turn the light on and immediately raise my face to the mirror over the small vanity.

Golden-blond hair tangled with white crust at my temple. Denim-blue eyes bloodshot with dark circles underneath. Purple marks on my throat and at my jaw.

"You're a real mess, Sela," I whisper to my reflection.

arre moment, I think she gives a sad nod of agree-
at me, but I blink hard. It's just me . . . the girl who
he attention and got it in all the wrong ways.

I grip the box cutter in my right hand, lower my face, and stare at it. My eyes flick to my left wrist and I see the purple bruises there that match the ones on my right. Slowly, I turn my left hand over, resting the back of it on the vanity. The pale skin of my wrist is exposed, the blue veins providing me a road map.

Taking the box cutter, I press the tip of the razor into my skin and look up into the mirror once more.

"You're a real mess," I tell myself again.

Then I push down with the blade.

CHAPTER 1

Sela

"Bring me a beer, will you?" Mark calls out to me.

I roll my eyes, turn around in midstride, and head back to the refrigerator. I open it up, grab a Bud, and bump the door closed with my hip before starting back to the living room.

"And the Doritos," he says. "I've got the munchies."

Another eye roll and I turn back around. Snatch the half-eaten bag of Doritos off the counter and head into the living room. As I round the couch, I toss the bag at him, catching him square in the chest. As he grabs his snackage, I hand him his beer. He takes it without even looking over at me, his eyes glued to the TV. One of those cheesy entertainment shows doing a piece on a movie star, athlete, or maybe a reality-show contestant just out of rehab and hawking their new bestselling book on how you can overcome addiction.

I plop onto the couch beside him, lean forward, and grab the large book off my coffee table.

Human Cognition.

Ugh.

"Are you going to study or just watch TV?" I ask as I open the text and flip to chapter 22.

"Watch TV," Mark says, his mouth full of Doritos and the air still sweetly perfumed from the bong he'd been smoking.

Mark's cute and all. We met several months ago at Golden Gate University, as both of us were starting in the MA Counseling Psychology program and there was an instant attraction, but the four-year age difference wears thin sometimes.

It took me a while to get my bachelor's degree. To say I was fucked in the head for quite a long time would be an understatement, what with my issues and all, plus a few psych hospitalizations. Add on my mom dying of an aneurysm three years ago, and I was the ripe age of twenty-five when I finally finished my bachelor's and started my master's last fall. I'm not exactly ancient now at twenty-six, but compared to Mark's twenty-two years, the differences in our priorities are glaring. Partying is still a big part of his life, and he doesn't take studying as seriously as I did. I clearly don't take smoking pot as seriously as he does.

But no biggie, really. I don't have enough of an emotional connection to care if he flunks. He's been good for a few laughs, and while sex with him is mediocre at best, he doesn't bother me too much. As with any man that I've been sexually involved with over the years, there is a mutually beneficial exchange. I let them use my body to get off, and they in turn make me feel as if I'm worthy to let them get off. It's this whole fucked-up, twisted reasoning I have in my head that no amount of psychological counseling has been able to straighten out so far. Our "friends with benefits" deal works out for the most part, except when he comes over, gets high, and then has Dorito breath. He sure as shit isn't getting any tonight the way things are going.

Just as well. I have to study for a big test tomorrow and I intend to pass it with flying colors, regardless if Mark does the same.

It's the end of my first year in the master's course and I'm halfway there. It's a goal I can't sacrifice.

I suck on the tiny ring pierced straight through the middle of my lower lip. A gift to myself when I got accepted into the program. It joins the matching two rings in my left eyebrow, and will hopefully be joined by a bridge piercing when I can muster up enough extra shifts at the diner to pay for it. Facial piercings have been my newest addiction; the sweet agony of metal punching through flesh feels oh so good to me. I was forced to move to the front of my face after both ears ran out of room.

Mark sets the Doritos on the couch next to him and wipes his orange fingers on his jeans. He takes a swallow of beer and places his left hand on my thigh. Leaning his head onto my shoulder, he says, "Want to fool around?"

I give a mighty shrug and dislodge him. "Not now."

"But I'm horny," he says with a whine.

Not attractive.

"You're always horny," I say as I try to concentrate on the first line of the chapter.

"You usually are too," he points out, hand moving up my thigh.

I roll my eyes, because that's not exactly true. I just accommodate whenever he's horny.

Whatever.

My gaze slides across the TV, past it, then notices something vaguely familiar before snapping right back to the screen.

A good-looking man who looks recognizable is being interviewed on TV. Charcoal-gray tailored suit, white dress shirt, and a pale blue tie. He flashes dimples in his grin as he talks to the reporter.

". . . the success of The Sugar Bowl has surpassed all of our expectations," he says with a twinkling eye. "It shows the world that there's a lot of room in our society for unconventional relationships."

The reporter, if she can be called that since this is an entertainment "news" channel, uncrosses and recrosses long, sexy legs in a short skirt. She tries to look hard-hitting when she leans forward in her chair, exposing more cleavage from a low-cut blouse, and asks, "But what about those opponents that say what you're doing is nothing more than prostitution?"

The man gives a charming laugh, picks at some imaginary lint on his leg, which is crossed in a dapper fashion over the other. "There is absolutely no money exchanged for sexual services. The Sugar Bowl does nothing more than charge a fee to our Sugar Daddies so they can join the website and make connections. None of the arrangements made thereafter are for sex; it's merely for companionship."

"But sex does occur," the reporter says silkily.

"Of course sex occurs," he admits with a languid smile. "People have sex. It makes the world go 'round."

The camera fades to black and then rolls to footage of a beach. It looks tropical in nature, as the water is crystal clear with a tinge of pale blue, and the sand is pristine white. The reporter's voice comes over the shot and says, "Jonathon Townsend is never shy to talk about sex, and by the looks of things, he gets plenty from the abundant supply of Sugar Babies that flock to his company daily."

The camera zooms in on a couple frolicking in the ocean. It's the man who was just being interviewed, wearing a pair of well-fit swim trunks on his muscular frame. A beautiful young woman with long blond hair wraps her arms around his neck as his hands go to her ass. As they kiss, the reporter's voice says, "It's rumored that Jonathon Townsend, or JT to his close personal friends, made an estimated eighteen million dollars last year in earnings from The Sugar Bowl, which certainly makes him more attractive than his already fine physique he recently showcased as he cavorted in the Maldives with his newest flame. With the service having over five million subscribers and still climbing at an astronomical rate, it's clear that JT's star is still on the rise."

JT?

My skin tightens and the hair on my arms stands on edge. The fingers on my right hand involuntarily seek my left wrist, rubbing lightly over the tiny, half-inch scar there that seems to throb in acknowledgment of something, but I'm not sure what.

My eyes are glued to the TV as I watch the man and woman kissing passionately, clearly not worried that they are on public display. Then he releases his hold on her, turns toward the camera with a smile on his face, and I see his torso.

Red bird.

Phoenix with flames at the wings and tail.

Stretched in flight up his left rib cage.

A shudder seizes my body and a surge of nausea hits me hard. I swallow against it as I lurch off the couch, awkwardly stumbling around the coffee table toward the TV. The camera zooms in closer on the couple, and as if the man known as Jonathon Townsend knows he's being watched, he looks right into the lens and grins, close enough that I can see his brown eyes.

Brown eyes. What I think might be filled with apology, but no . . . that's malice. Evil, taunting malice.

"Damn, baby . . . sorry . . . looks like we left some spunk in your hair," he says with a jeering laugh.

I cry out, stumble backward, and the coffee table catches the backs of my knees, causing me to fall down hard on it. My right hand grips my left wrist, the scar now shrieking in agony.

"Sela . . . you okay?" Mark says, his voice sounding like it's stuffed into a drum and sealed tight because the blood is rushing through my head with such force it's blocking other noise.

"Get out," I whisper, choking on the words because my throat is so dry.

"What?" I hear him rise from the couch, see his legs rounding the coffee table in my periphery.

I raise my head, look at him, and rasp, "Get out."

"You want me to leave? Right now?"

Red-hot rage swells up within me and I screech at him as I lunge upward from the table, my fists balled up in fury, "Get out. Get out. Get out."

Mark jerks backward from me, his eyes round with surprise for just a moment before they harden. He reaches down, grabs his backpack off the floor, and mutters, "Crazy bitch."

I don't even look at him again as he walks out of my small apartment.

My hands come to my temples and pull at my hair, fisting hard and jerking. I pace back and forth in front of the TV, my eyes cutting to it periodically, but they've moved on to another juicy story.

Vivid flashes of scenes spark in my brain. Scenarios I've seen before in nightmares but thought they were nothing but nightmares.

My wrists pinned to the mattress.

Searing pain as I'm fucked in the ass.

Red phoenix on a wrist.

"Think she'll suck my dick?"

"Swallow it."

"All of it."

I bend over at the waist, my stomach cramping violently, then a flood of vomit shoots out of my mouth. I hurl loudly, groaning as wave after wave of nausea and pain are expelled from my body. Beer and the turkey sandwich I'd eaten twenty minutes ago splatter loudly on my worn brown carpet. Tears flood my vision, drip in rivers onto the pile of vomit as I start to dry heave.

Dropping to my knees, I heave and gag, my hands coming to rest at the sides of the gelatinous pile of grief soaking into my carpet. My nose starts running freely now, snot adding to the vile mixture.

I suck in air, deep into my lungs, and will my heart to stop its mad beating of terror. The urge to slice into my healed scar overwhelms me, terrifies me so badly I start sobbing. That is something I cannot do again. Those days are over.

Minutes pass by as I stay on my hands and knees, hunched over the sickness on my floor. My breathing starts to calm down, my heart rate slowly falls back into the range of normal. I lift a hand, drag the back of it over my snotty nose, then wipe it on my jeans. Clumsily, I push myself up off the floor and consider the ramifications of what I just saw.

Of what I just remembered.

My rapist. One of them at least.

Good-looking golden boy sitting on some type of empire and vacationing in the Maldives.

Does he even remember what he did to me?

"Swallow it. All of it."

A flash of furious indignation boils my blood and I go dizzy for a moment, realizing that while my life fell apart following that night, his only got better and better. He walked on my back . . . a straight path to success. Took my innocence in more ways than one, and told me he made all my fantasies come true.

Something black and oily starts to fill my chest. Permeates my entire being. A dark shadowing so viscous, it starts to cloud my vision and I think momentarily I might be going blind.

Hatred. White hot and boiling my insides painfully.

A sickly pervasive need to cut myself, which causes more shame and humiliation.

". . . looks like we left some spunk in your hair."

I swallow against the vomit rising up within me again. I had thought I was past all this shit. Figured I'd finally gotten my life together, and while I may not have made ultimate peace with what happened, because apparently I just can't forgive myself for my part in all of it, I was moving on. I was learning to get through the nightmares and, even though I abhor intimacy, I was at least giving sex a try so I could feel somewhat normal.

And that fucker . . . he's taken all of that away from me. All my little baby steps of progress and the slight amount of strength I've been able to muster to continue living life to some extent. All within the blink of an eye, Jonathon Townsend has taken that all away from me, and while my wrist may not be bleeding at this very moment, I feel like I'm back at square one.

How can I possibly overcome this?

What could I possibly do to make this better for me?

How in the fuck do I stop hurting?

And then it comes to me immediately.

Almost too easy.

Just one word, very simple and yet so very right.

Murder.

It flashes over and over again; sharp electrical pulses burning themselves into my brain. I know, without a doubt, there's only one thing that will make this right for me.

I'm going to make Jonathon Townsend pay for what he did to me.

CHAPTER 2

Beck

I flip from screen to screen, navigating the new beta site for The Sugar Bowl. My programmers have been working nonstop for the last six months to roll out this new platform that provides a better search engine, a more robust communication interface, and the ability to video chat between the Sugar Daddies and Sugar Babies. Of course, we also had to program in some type of quality assurance on the video plug-in to assure that the chats are clean and nonpornographic.

That's the problem when you own a company that pairs men and women for a relationship that's not supposed to be based on sex but most assuredly is. Sure . . . there are some Sugar Daddies who are probably too old to get it up but still want the pretty girl on their arm, and I'm sure in those few circumstances, it's purely platonic.

But for the most part, Sugar Daddies not only want the pretty girl on their arm, they want them flat on their back in their bed, or hunched over their lap in the back of their limousines sucking on their cock.

That's really what the Sugar Daddies pay for.

I know it.

JT knows it.

The world knows it.

We just ensure no money changes hands for the expectation of sex, and we avert any trouble with the law. This was something we spent months having a legal team analyze before we even put the venture capital to use in building the business. No way was JT about to sink millions into an enterprise that could collapse with criminal indictments.

The phone on my desk chimes and my secretary's voice comes over the speaker. "Beck . . . there's a young lady here to see you. She doesn't have an appointment."

"What's she want?" I ask as I pull up the beta chat screen and type a test message to one of my programmers.

Fuck, but I miss doing the actual programming. This is my original baby before my eyes. Sure, it's morphed to become better and better, but it's all my vision. While my fingers may not actually be punching in the coding sequences anymore, I'm still actively involved in the design, theory, and testing. It's just that now, one floor down in our San Francisco offices, that's done by a team of fresh young programmers straight out of Stanford, MIT, or other equally prestigious schools.

"It's a Baby," Linda says quietly, her voice full of grandmotherly affection. She calls all the Sugar Babies just Baby. "I think you need to meet with her."

Christ. I don't need this shit again. I hear it in Linda's voice. I know exactly why there's a Baby here and I don't even need to talk to her to know that I'll be paying a very angry visit to JT soon.

"Send her in," I say as I log out of the beta program and stand up from my desk.

The door to my office opens and Linda escorts a young woman

in. Exactly JT's type. Blond, built, and innocent-looking. While all of our Sugar Babies are eighteen or older, this girl looks like she could pass for fifteen, which is another thing that JT looks for in his acquisitions.

I step forward, hold out my hand. "I'm Beckett North, but everyone just calls me Beck."

Her eyes are frightened and I can see the hint of a bruise at the base of her throat. My stomach recoils as I accept her hand. It's soft, delicate, and weak in my grip. She's subservient, just the way JT likes them.

"Jenny Warlick," she says softly. My eyes cut past the girl to Linda, who gives me a sad smile, backs out of my office, and closes the door.

I release her hand and wave to the couch. My office is so large it affords ample space for my U-shaped work desk that holds four computer monitors, a small round table with four chairs, and a seating area that boasts a couch and two sumptuous chairs. A liquor bar is built into one wall, but I don't offer her a drink other than water or soda. She declines.

Jenny takes a seat on the couch and I sit in one of the chairs opposite with a low coffee table in between us.

"So tell me what's wrong," I say after we get settled in.

I'm so fucking pissed at JT my hands are shaking. I make my way down the long hallway that separates our corner offices and practically bark at his secretary when I reach her desk. "Is he in?"

"Yes, but he doesn't want to be dist—"

I ignore her, throw open JT's office door so hard it bangs against the interior wall like a thunderclap. I find him hunched over his desk, snorting a line of coke.

"Fucking typical," I growl as I slam the door closed behind

me, which probably only ensures his secretary now has her ear pressed against the door.

His head raises up slowly and he takes a deep sniff, his eyes bloodshot and watery.

Pupils dilated to pinpricks.

"You fucking asshole," I grit out as I stalk up to his desk. "You're fucking doing blow in your office now?"

"Relax," he says with a grin, running a finger under his nose to wipe the residue away. "It's just a pick-me-up. I had a late night last night."

"With Jenny Warlick," I snarl. "She just left my office."

"Who?" he asks dumbly, and I have to physically restrain myself from punching him.

"The girl you fucked last night. Tied to your bed. There's fucking bruises on her neck, you asshole, and she's scared."

JT shrugs and says, "Huh. Don't really remember."

"Because you were probably high," I shoot back.

"Probably," he says with carefree aplomb. "But relax . . . I'll drop some money in her account. That's all these girls want."

"You cannot give her money for sex, you idiot." My fingers curl into fists and I can feel my blood hammering so hard the pulse in my neck is thumping. "And you're lucky she's not crying rape."

"She wasn't raped," JT says as he leans back in his chair and puts his hands behind his head. "She willingly let me tie her up. Hell, she came on to me. They all want a piece of the king Daddy."

"Thought you didn't remember," I grit out, but it's futile.

He remembers enough, probably more so because last night was his normal modus operandi. And I came on strong throwing out the *rape* word to JT, but I wanted to try to scare him. Jenny never even implied that to me, and even confirmed what he just said. She let him tie her up, but she was scared because he got rougher than what she had expected. He told Jenny last night he wanted to see her again, but she wants no part of that and came to me because she's worried it's going to hurt her status as a Sugar Baby with the company. I, of course, assured her it would not and that JT wouldn't expect anything further from her.

Fuck, but he's gotten so out of control these last few months since the news outlets started reporting on our business. He loves the limelight and the stardom. Loves the endless stream of pussy in his bed and people bowing down to his greatness.

Always seeking the next big rush. The thrill that will make that last orgasm pale in comparison. He's using drugs and making stupid business decisions, and Jenny isn't the first one to come to me that has been roughed up by JT. My respect for him is all but destroyed and I just don't have it in me to continue on like this, despite my tie to him.

"I want to buy you out," I tell him in a calm, level voice.

That gets his attention and the smug smile slides from his face. He sniffs deeply and leans forward in his chair. "Absolutely not."

"This isn't working," I tell him. "We've diverged on how we want to run this business."

"My business," he says flatly.

"No . . . it's our business. It's fifty-fifty."

"I provided the start-up and capital—"

"I provided the product. Without my skills, The Sugar Bowl wouldn't have even come into existence. And I'm not arguing with your coked-out ass. We have the partnership papers to prove my worth, so I repeat . . . I want to buy you out. We can get a trio of appraisers to value The Sugar Bowl. You choose one, I'll choose one, and they'll choose an independent. Come up with a fair price, and I'll pay you the money. You can walk and go start up some other business if you want."

Or just live on the interest earnings and fuck your way through the free world, I think to myself, because JT's done. My friend, through childhood and beyond, is but a pale shadow. My tie to him runs deeper than anyone can begin to imagine. Deeper than JT could even imagine, and yet I feel it all slipping away. The suave and intelligent businessman I knew and partnered up with three years ago is gone. Not a shred left of the man I'd respected, although never really admired. He was often sort of a douche.

"Not doing it," he says adamantly, and I sigh in frustration.

"I can force a buyout," I threaten.

"Go ahead," he says, calling my bluff. "You know our agreement's loaded with protective clauses for me. You'll never get the company, but tell you what . . . you want out, I'll buy *you* out. Programmers like you are a dime a dozen."

I grit my teeth so violently, I'm afraid the enamel will crack. JT turns his chair back to his desk and proceeds to cut another line. I've been dismissed.

"What happened to you, man?" I ask softly, searching for a hint of the good I know is inside of him.

His head snaps up and he blinks those bloodshot eyes. "What do you mean?"

"I mean *what in the fuck happened to you?* You were a brilliant businessman, the world was your oyster. Now you're partying with a terrible crowd, scaring women, and you're making some piss-poor financial decisions. You're on a spiral, JT, and you're bringing everything down with you."

He stares at me a moment, taking in the hard set to my jaw, the worry in my eyes . . . the defeat in my shoulders. His own eyes soften, relaxing the fine lines and giving him a more youthful look. Almost like the JT of old.

"Listen," he says in a conciliatory tone as he stands from his desk. He walks around it, throws an arm over my shoulder. "We're like brothers. Buds for life and then after. I appreciate your concern, but I've got things under control. I swear it."

Truth and lies.

Yes, we're like brothers and actually are fraternity brothers. We were friends even before that, having attended the same prep school. Our families are intertwined through money and social status. As far as being buds for life, not sure about that one. It's a lie he's got things under control, but I hold my peace. It won't do any good to argue with him.

No, I think my next conversation needs to be with an attorney to figure out if there's a way for me to get out of this clusterfuck and cut JT cleanly out of my life. I think it's time to let him go.

With The Sugar Bowl firmly in my sole possession.

CHAPTER 3

Sela

I look in the mirror, still shocked with my new appearance.

Six months ago, I ditched every bit of metal in my face and ears except a hole in each lobe that now sports tiny gold hoops. I'm lucky everything closed up nicely with barely perceptible scarring. I cut friendship ties with Mark and the handful of others, making my life more solitary than normal. I joined a gym, spent my precious money on a trainer, and got rid of twenty pounds that were seemingly welded onto my lower stomach, ass, and hips. I spent even more precious money by coloring my golden blond hair a rich, chocolate brown—eyebrows too—and now my blue eyes sizzle like electric orbs. The dusting of freckles across my nose and cheeks also stands out against the dark hair, and I find I like the look. I'm like a slightly younger version of Jennifer Garner but without the bangs.

Innocent and fresh. Two words that should never be used to describe the dark and damaged woman I've become.

My last step to transformation included a full wax, because I didn't want blond pubes giving away my disguise. It was painful but necessary, should I find myself in a position to take my disguise that far.

I am ready.

I wash my hands and look into the bathroom mirror.

"You can do this," I murmur to myself, remembering a time ten years ago that I stared into a mirror just before slicing open my wrist. "You can totally do this, Sela."

Infiltrate.

Murder.

Repeat.

It's a simple plan, really.

I give a quick scan of my makeup and deem it perfect. I had to have someone teach me, because I never wore this crap before. Never cared about my looks or catching a man's attention.

Until now.

Now I'm getting ready to step out into the ballroom of the Four Seasons hotel and put myself on display. My dark hair falling in lustrous waves over bare shoulders, my skimpy dress and ridiculous heels I spent weeks practicing in, and a sexy attitude I also practiced, all in the hopes of catching Jonathon Townsend's eye.

Six months ago, I hurled on my living room carpet.

Within minutes of that, I developed a plan for justice.

It's taken me a long time to get here, but now today is the first day of the rest of my new life. It's where I'm going to make things right for poor Sela Halstead.

I'm going to make *him* suffer and then I'm going to end him.

My nefarious plan is quite easy, at least to my way of thinking that admittedly might be colored by an overabundance of rage and an overwhelming need for retribution. After only a few hours of Internet research, I had all I needed to know about my rapist.

Jonathon Townsend, age thirty-two.

Attended Hillcrest Preparatory. Bachelor's and MBA from Stanford.

Wealthy by birth. Spoiled by circumstance.

Launched The Sugar Bowl three years ago and made millions upon millions.

Playboy. Bachelor. Rapist.

Those are the basics, and I find it hilariously ironic that his own business is going to be my way in to him. My research on The Sugar Bowl was fastidious and there were dozens of articles about it. CNN even did a documentary about the revolutionary and unconventional website platform that hooked up Sugar Daddies with Sugar Babies.

Quite brilliant, actually.

Sugar Daddies are wealthy men, usually in their fifties and sixties, who are looking to regain their youth by dating much younger women. Beautiful women too. Now there are some more youthful Sugar Daddies, but they are few and far between and obviously in high demand. I wondered why the vast majority of Sugar Daddies were old enough to be grandfathers, but according to the CNN film, most wealthy men in their thirties and forties were trying out the family life with cute suburban wives and a passel of kids. It's usually not until divorce hits and the resulting fat belly sets in that these guys start scrambling to prove their manhood. Statistically speaking, that most often happens in a man's late forties after the kids are grown and the wife doesn't give it up anymore.

The Sugar Bowl makes all of this easy for these poor, ignored men by providing a database of willing Sugar Babies.

Sugar Babies are young women, usually between eighteen and twenty-six, although some can be a bit older. CNN says the average age is actually twenty-two, and that's because most Sugar Babies are joining as a means to get their college tuition paid. At twenty-six, I'm stretching the outer limit of the normal range, but my face is very youthful and I could pass for twenty if I wanted.

While most sugarships—that's a combination of "sugar" and "relationships"—are formed through introductions facilitated through the Web database, much like some of the popular dating sites, The Sugar Bowl also hosts regional parties where the Daddies and the Babies can mix, mingle, and have face-to-face time to see if there are any common bonds.

What's the typical "sugarship" look like?

Well, there's actually a written contract. In a signed agreement, all expectations are laid out. The Sugar Daddy clearly defines what he wants from his Baby. It could be a live-in companion or someone to travel with. It could be as simple as just a weekly dinner date. In return, the Daddy promises the Baby certain things. That could be money, tuition expenses, a car, expensive jewelry, whatever.

Bottom line: the Daddy pays for the Baby.

One thing you will never find in the agreement is an expectation to have sex. In fact, after I joined The Sugar Bowl two weeks ago, it was interesting to read their sample agreement online and find that it actually has a clause that "specifically prohibits discussion and/or agreement regarding sexual acts in exchange for monetary compensation and/or gifts."

Squeaky-clean on its face, but as CNN showed during the documentary, sex is most often implied. Numerous former Sugar Babies were interviewed. Most of them were very happy with their experiences, having come out of college debt-free. Most of them also admitted that sex was a given and were unapologetic about having their expenses paid in return for a little roll between the sheets.

I find it sickening and repulsive, and yet . . . here I am. Getting ready to attend a San Francisco Sugar Bowl Mixer, and I have it on good authority from Jonathon Townsend's secretary, Karla Gould, that he's going to be here. I'm not the least bit ashamed that I researched and targeted her as an unwilling accomplice in my plans. I learned that she's thirty-three, divorced, a single mom of three, and desperate for friends. I ultimately stalked her, forming a friendship after a "chance meeting" in her favorite coffee shop. That happened two months ago, and I played up my down-on-my-luck poor college student trying to pay for her master's degree, which led to Karla suggesting The Sugar Bowl to me. While she's too old and too overweight to be a marketable Baby, she had no problem with urging me in that direction, and I did a great acting job looking surprised at the suggestion, slightly dubious yet equally intrigued.

Karla was a good inside source, and I even once met her at her office for lunch and got a peek inside the great Jonathon Townsend's empty office. I almost shuddered in ecstasy as I imagined jamming a letter opener through his eye and deep into his brain while he sat at his desk and computed his millions.

My plan is simple, and as such, will involve a great deal of luck.

I am going to try to catch Jonathon Townsend's attention tonight. It's well-known that he prefers blondes, but it's also well known he prefers big tits, and I have a set of those. My blond hair is not an option, because I don't want him to recognize me.

I don't think he will, because I have learned in my research that he's an egomaniac. I also learned that he fucks a lot of blondes and I have to imagine all of our faces blend together. While I can't be sure, I'm betting on his cocky arrogance and the fact it probably had him forgetting about me even before the semen in my hair dried that night.

Rage sparks, froths, and bubbles low in my gut as I think about it.

Infiltrate.

Murder.

Repeat.

Keep your eyes on the prize, Sela.

Infiltrate . . . get Townsend's attention tonight. Make him lust after you. Get him to take you to his house. Make him divulge the other two rapists' names, which shouldn't be a problem inducing him to do that given the gun in my purse.

Murder . . . easy enough. Bullet between the eyes.

Repeat . . . find the other two and stalk them. Bullets between their eyes as well.

I stare at myself in the mirror just a moment more, taking in the smoky eyes, plump and glossed lips, cleavage on full display. I know what I'm doing is rash, probably not the most airtight of plans, but I can't help it. I have rage and hate driving me forward. Even if I get caught and spend the rest of my life in prison, it will be better than living with myself having not done anything at all.

Watch out, Mr. Townsend. Your time is almost up.

CHAPTER 4

Beck

As much as I sneer at JT's overusage of the Babies available, I have to admit, it's one of the perks of ownership. While the mission of the The Sugar Bowl is to help facilitate meaningful and companionable relationships—or sugarships as some freak in the marketing department dubbed them—I tend to pick from the eager stock intent on only one-night stands.

I may be richer than God at this point in my life, but I have no desire to pay for some college sweetie to move into my bedroom just so I can have the assurance of someone playing with my balls every night. Instead, I found out soon enough that most of these women are so hungry in their quest for achievement they'll set their eyes on the top dogs and will pin all their hopes on just one shot at them.

They have an ulterior motive and I don't hold that against them. Sugar Babies are beautiful, smart, and calculating. Most would make tremendous businesswomen. But they have an agenda, and so do I. They are seeking a windfall in the form of money, and perhaps a lasting connection. I may own the company that makes this possible for them, but I'm in no form or fashion a

Sugar Daddy myself. I have no need of relationships, and while I have the utmost respect for women, even those who are cool with my desire only for a one-night stand, I can't see that changing anytime soon for me.

So yes, I take advantage of this fucking spectacular perk of owning The Sugar Bowl. I get a hot-as-hell fuck with no strings attached, and the best part is, at the end of the night, I can slink out of whatever room we're occupying . . . hotel, public restroom, back of my limo . . . and not have to look at starry eyes in the morning hoping that I'll wise up and offer marriage to the young beauty in my bed.

Because let's face it . . . that's what these Sugar Babies want. While their immediate goals might be stability and financial gain, they all have the same long-term outlook. Every one of them is hoping to catch a rich man who will keep them swimming in jewels and furs forever.

And good for them. Use what you have, girl, and work it hard. Just don't flash that shit my way, as I'm not about to give up my independence to commitment.

My gaze wanders around the ballroom. These Sugar Bowl mixers are opulent and flashy, giving the Babies a taste of the decadence that awaits them. Caviar and champagne. Thousand-dollar suits. Wristwatches that cost more than cars. They take it all in with wide-eyed innocence, and they spread their legs a little farther to entice a Daddy to notice them.

I've seen it all before.

See it happening right now all over this room as the women flirt, suck on lower lips, and pull their dresses down just a little more to expose their cleavage. The room is thick with lust pouring off the men who see nothing but orgasms in their immediate future after going so long without. The girls see dollar signs. It's a mutually beneficial relationship.

Taking a sip from my drink as I stand at the bar, I glance down to my left. Several couples are sitting on stools, drinking cocktails and making small talk. At the very end sits a woman who is strikingly lovely. Her back is to the bar, the stool swiveled so she can face the mingling crowd. A shimmery silver dress hugs her curves, and I lean back from the bar so I can get a better look at knockout stiletto sandals with silver ribbon at the heels that wind up and around her calves.

Pulling my body back in, I take another look at her face. It's in profile to me, but she's all gorgeous angles and soft curves. Straight nose, high cheekbones, and full, puffy lips. Dark chocolate-brown hair, and I wonder what color her eyes are, but I can't see from this position.

She seems to be staring at something intently so I turn my head and follow her line of sight across the room.

Ahhh . . . there it is.

She's staring at JT, who is standing with three women huddled around him, all vying for his attention. I look back at the brunette sitting at the bar and find her stare a bit disconcerting. It's not hungry or calculating; not the way I've seen women look at me and my partner before. Instead, she looks sort of angry.

Odd.

Jealous former Baby, perhaps?

I start to put it out of my mind because that's a complication I don't need, but just as I begin to turn away, she pushes up off the stool, squares her shoulders, and starts to cross the room toward JT.

She has a sexy as hell walk, full of confidence as her hips sway. Her breasts aren't bound by a bra under the shimmery dress and they sway in full natural glory. What I wouldn't love to do to a pair of tits like that, and an image of me fucking said tits crosses my mind.

I watch with interest to see what happens, because while I don't like confrontation, I wouldn't mind watching JT get a comeuppance if that's what's on the brunette's mind. Or maybe an old-fashioned catfight between her and the blondes that might involve hair pulling and an errant kick to JT's nuts. He'd so deserve it.

Fucking JT.

I've got my attorney reading over our partnership agreement, poring over case law, trying to figure out if I have a way to force him out, but so far it doesn't look good. So my choices are going to be stay the course and hope JT gets his head out of his ass, or let him buy me out and walk. It's an option, but not the best, as I've got a lot of pride invested in this business. Do I have the smarts to make a killing off another start-up? Hell, yes. But I'm not ready to give up this ride yet because it could be so much more, and besides . . . maybe JT is just going through a phase. Maybe he'll wise up sooner rather than later and this will all be moot.

God, I hope to fuck he comes to his senses, because JT and I have history together. Deep ties that I don't want to sever if it can be helped. While I might not like him at the moment, I still hold out hope that he can be pulled back from the edge.

The brunette reaches JT's group and I watch as his eyes connect with hers. He lowers his gaze, runs his eyes all over her body, because hell . . . who wouldn't? She's stunning.

When his eyes meets hers again, she boldly steps in between two of the blondes and holds her hand out to him. While I can't hear anything because of the chatter of about two hundred people and soft strains of some techno dance music, I can imagine her bold introduction. I bet her voice is smoky . . . filled with sex.

JT inclines his head toward her in polite acknowledgment and releases her hand, turning his gaze back to the blonde who is now hanging on his left arm. He dips his head to her and she presses her lips near his ear, I'm sure offering to do any dirty thing imaginable he desires, and I know the brunette won't be looked at again.

Not only does she not have the right hair color, but she screwed up when she approached JT. He likes his women docile and subservient. Her confident strut, I'm betting firm handshake, and direct approach turned him off. Not that he wouldn't fuck her if there was nothing else available, but for the most part . . . her type doesn't do it for him.

Her type, however, does a shitload for me. I like my women confident and feisty in bed. I like a good tussle when the mood suits us both, and I want her screaming at me to go harder because she wants it, not just because I like to give it. I like a woman to look me directly in the eye when she's sucking my cock, and I'm betting this woman would do just that.

The brunette continues to stare at JT, and I notice with a small amount of surprise her fingers curled into fists that are clenched tightly. Maybe she'll deck him, which won't be as good as a swift kick in the balls, but would still be entertaining.

Instead, she turns from the group and her shoulders sag in what I'd consider to be defeat. Her head is still held high though, and when she angles my way, I can see the clear blue of her eyes even across the dim room.

Just fucking stunning, and JT's all kinds of a fool to let that get away.

But his loss is my gain, and I push away from the bar to intercept her.

We meet in the middle of the ballroom, her eyes widening in surprise as she realizes I'm intent on talking to her. I see almost a subtle hint of a wall going up and her shoulders tighten.

"Don't take it personally," I tell her with a charming smile as

I take her by the elbow, guiding her to the bar where I left my drink. "He doesn't like confident women. Threatens his masculinity and all."

She gives an unladylike snort. "I find that hard to believe."

Yes! A smoky voice that sounds exactly like sex. I knew it.

"Well, it's true, and I know him better than anyone in this room," I tell her truthfully as we reach the bar and I pull out a stool for her. "Let me get you a drink and I'll tell you all about it."

She sits down, crosses one smooth leg over the other, and looks me directly in the face. "So . . . are you going to divulge all of your partner's dirty secrets to me, Mr. North?"

Ahhhh . . . she does know who I am.

"It's just Beck," I reply as I hold my hand out to her. She takes it and rather than shake, I pull it up to my lips and press a whisper of a kiss on her knuckles. "You know who I am?"

"Techie mastermind of The Sugar Bowl," she says with a shrug, and I don't see a hint of calculation in her eyes. Instead, she says, "I'm Sela Halstead, and I was hoping to get a moment with Mr. Townsend to talk about The Sugar Bowl."

My stomach bottoms out a bit, because I hate deception, and I eyeball her shrewdly. "You don't look like a reporter."

She gives a husky laugh and touches her fingertips to my forearm in reassurance. "No. I'm a Sugar Baby, but I am writing a paper in my psych class about the sexual evolution of the human mind. I thought he'd have some interesting perspectives to share."

The tension leaves my shoulders and I smile at her. "Well, I'm sure I could provide you with the same type of information you're looking for. I'm well versed on sexual evolution and my mind is quite human."

She laughs again and I raise my hand to catch the bartender's attention. I look back down at her and ask, "What are you drinking?"

She stares at me a moment, chews on her bottom lip as if plagued with indecision. Her eyes cut across the room to JT and then back to me before she finally says, "Whatever you're serving at your place."

CHAPTER 5

Sela

I'll have to say, the photographs I'd seen of Beck North don't do him justice.

In researching Jonathon Townsend, I'd naturally read my fill about his friend and business partner, Beckett North. While he chooses to stay out of the limelight for the most part, there was still a wealth of biographical information to be found.

He'd attended the same prep school as Townsend and also went to Stanford. But whereas JT went on to pursue an MBA at his alma mater, Beck went east and got his master's in computer science at MIT. He's hailed by some as a certified genius, while others wonder why he wasted his talents on building a Web-based platform that was nothing more than another dating site. Regardless, my research showed well enough that Beck North was the brains behind this venture, while JT was the rich, pretty face they put on the posters.

Except, in my humble opinion, Beck North is infinitely more gorgeous than Jonathon Townsend, and that has nothing to do with my bias and hate toward my rapist.

Beck North is starring perfection in every woman's fantasy. Tall, broad shoulders that fill out his expensively tailored suit in such a way that you know he was born to a life of privilege. Yet his eyes, which are more aquamarine than blue, hold a certain amount of humbleness within them. Whereas JT's gaze was filled with nothing but condescension and arrogance, Beck's is friendly and charming.

There's no doubt he's probably sporting a four-hundred-dollar haircut as his dark brown hair is short on the sides, longer on the top with stylishly messy spikes pushed up and away from his forehead. Beck North oozes sophistication and smarts that would enable him to walk into any Wall Street boardroom and command attention. This is a product of his birth, social status, elite schooling, and multimillionaire ranking. In this respect, he and JT are just alike.

But there was a glaring difference as I read about the two co-founders of The Sugar Bowl. Most of the articles and pictures of JT showcased a man who lived the high life. Ate at the most expensive restaurants, had the most lavish vacations, and frivolously spent his money on stupid shit like underwater personal submarines and advance seating on the first personal spaceship to the moon.

Despite the nearly identical upbringing and social status, Beck North is a completely different story. Most articles about him dealt with his philanthropic and charitable work, his main passions including equal educational opportunities for inner-city kids and disaster-recovery work. I found numerous pictures of him in sweat-soaked and mud-covered clothes assisting disaster victims in the cleanup process. Find a hurricane, tornado, typhoon, mudslide, or tsunami in the world, and Beck North was jetting off to help clean up. I saw he was once quoted as saying, "I've always been a hard worker, but let's face it. I sit at a desk all day in the air-conditioning. This is just a good way to get my hands dirty and keep my ego in check."

There was another difference as well. While most articles of JT showed him with a gorgeous beauty on his arm at every celebrity event he attended, Beck never seemed to date anyone. He always went stag to the few public events he attended, and I even read an article that said he was too busy with his career to have time for a relationship. He didn't say this in a cold demeanor, but merely in a matter-of-fact way that told you love was low on his list of priorities.

So what I've read about this enigmatic man makes it easy for me to believe that while most of his life is probably spent in boardrooms, because of his easygoing charm and egoless attitude, I bet you could throw a pair of jeans and a T-shirt on him and he'd just as easily fit into a dive bar listening to a grunge band.

It was fascinating to read about him. Even more intriguing being up close.

But I'm not interested in him in any way other than trying to figure out in this moment how I can use him to achieve my goals. I'm clearly not going home with Jonathon Townsend tonight, as that little part of my plan that was dependent on luck that went south in a hurry. I knew the plan was rash, somewhat ridiculous, but it was only my first shot at JT. I never intended to give up if the first go-round came up empty.

"Whatever you're serving at your place," I told him as my blue eyes held his own. I had figured out enough in about thirty seconds that he likes the direct approach, unlike his partner.

Beck gives little in the way of surprise. Possibly a momentary lifting of his eyebrows over my bold offer, but instantly his eyes project an appreciative intensity that he very much likes my answer.

"Then let's go," he says as he takes my hand and suavely helps me right back off the barstool.

I made a command decision and I'm going with it. JT was a bust tonight, effectively shutting me down within seconds of my introduction. Beck confirmed for me what I figured out in those dismissive moments. Jonathon Townsend is intimidated by confident women. I miscalculated that, figuring the thrill for him was in bringing a woman such as that down. I mean, isn't that why rapists rape? For control, domination, and to compensate for all their mommy issues?

Thus, the minute Beck North confirmed for me the reason why I was snubbed this evening, I figured out that unless I'm willing to pull my gun out right here, right now, and murder Townsend with a few hundred witnesses, I need to take a step back and recalculate. Figure out a different way to go about this.

Besides, I can't go in for the quick kill. I need information from him first, which means I have to get close to him.

And perhaps Beck North is exactly what I need. Maybe an in with him will get me close to JT, but not so close as to risk exposure. Maybe I could even work something out that is less messy that the "bullet between the eyes" plan, which makes my stomach turn a bit. I'm not good with blood.

Maybe poison.

That's so much more stealthy and something I had actually considered before. Maybe I can get close to Townsend through Beck and then poison JT at an opportune moment. Of course, that would mean I'd have to give up my quest for the identity of my other rapists, so that might not work out after all. Besides . . .

I've been really looking forward to the instant gratification of watching fear overwhelm JT when I hold a gun to his head and then listen to him plead for his life. I won't get that with the poisoning option, but I've got a far better chance of getting away with murder that way.

This will take a bit more thought.

Maybe having Beck intervene is a godsend. Maybe it was a signal to me that I need to take a step back, cool down a bit, and go forth with a plan that is less rash and driven by emotion. I should be a bit more calculating and give up on the satisfaction I'd get from brains blowing out of his skull.

Yes . . . the gorgeous cofounder of The Sugar Bowl is probably exactly what I need.

I'm led out of the ballroom with a gentle hand on my elbow. Beck doesn't make small talk, but then why would he? My offer was clear, and it wasn't for a drink.

When we reach the elevators, he pushes the button and merely says, "I booked a room here tonight."

"That's convenient," I say with a laugh.

It's an easy laugh, and one I'm able to give with no qualms.

If you think I should be feeling uncertain or weirded out by the prospect of having sex with a complete stranger I met less than five minutes ago, you'd be wrong, because there is nothing I wouldn't do to carry out my plans.

Infiltrate.

Murder.

Repeat.

I will never be deterred in my revenge, and Beck North, with his good looks and brainy charm, is not going to be a chore for me at all.

The elevator door opens and Beck's hand drops from my

elbow and takes hold of mine, lacing his fingers throughout. It's an intimate act and my first reaction is to pull away, because intimacy has no place within my framework of deception. I need to remain cold and distanced, my mind focused on the ultimate goal.

And yet, his warm hand engulfing mine sends a tiny pulse of security through me.

Almost as if I have a partner in crime?

Or perhaps it's just a feeling of being grounded at this moment?

Let's face it, not but five minutes ago, my plan was to have this evening end in murder. Now it looks like it's going to end in sex with a very gorgeous man and a restructuring of my agenda.

As soon as the doors whisper closed and Beck hits the button for the thirteenth floor, he steps into me. With one hand still holding my own, and another pushed up under my chin to ensure my eyes lock with his, he tells me, "I'm not a Sugar Daddy, just so you know."

I blink at him in surprise, my mind spinning over the implications. "What do you mean?"

His voice is soft but firm. "What I mean is that while I'm one of the owners of The Sugar Bowl, and while you are a Sugar Baby, I am not a Sugar Daddy. I am not looking to commit my time to *one* woman, nor my resources to *any* woman. So if you're going up with me right now with the expectation that this will result in a lucrative contract, I'm going to have to disappoint you."

Well, fuck.

I was sort of banking on that being a definite possibility. I mean, the whole point of these mixers is to hook up and form relationships. I assumed that's why Beck was here. I thought it was sort of implied when he approached me. I mean, I didn't think it was a given that would occur, but I figured maybe a night of wild and freaky sex would make him inclined to want to keep me around for a bit. Even if it was for a short contract period like a month. That would have certainly given me the time to come up with a new plan to kill JT.

"Want me to take you back down?" Beck murmurs, and I blink again, trying to put my head in the game. The elevator comes to a stop and the doors slide open.

Time for another command decision and I go with my gut instinct. I've already figured out Beck likes a challenge, so I'm going to go with that.

"I didn't come tonight hoping to find a Sugar Daddy," I say truthfully. Because I didn't. I came to kill JT.

And then I tell him another truth, because when I decided that becoming a Sugar Baby was going to be my cover, I went all in and started talking to various men in case someone got suspicious of me. "I really came to try to meet Mr. Townsend for my paper. I'm actually in talks with a potential Sugar Daddy in Santa Clara and we're hoping to meet soon. He's looking for a long-term commitment, and I'm looking for something stable enough to carry me all the way through my master's degree."

This surprises him and his hand drops from my face. "Then why are you coming to my room with me?"

"Because until I do enter into a 'sugarship'—which is a stupid name, by the way—I'm a free agent. And I very much enjoy sex. Even more so with an intelligent, witty, and gorgeous man. So why not?"

Okay, so that was a lie about the enjoying sex part. My rapists ensured I'd never be comfortable with the act of sex, and so I only view it as a necessary function that serves some other purpose for me.

Beck's lips curve up and his eyes crinkle in silent amusement. "I like that answer very much, Miss Halstead."

"Good," I say with a wink, a little surprised with how well I've got my confident seductress act going. "Then let's get going."

His hand takes mine again and we walk from the elevator side by side. His room is at the end of the hallway, and when we enter, I see why. It's a corner suite with sweeping views of the Golden Gate Bridge and an outdoor balcony.

"Want a drink?" he asks as he lets my hand go and loosens his tie.

"No, I'm good," I say as I look around, taking a few steps toward the balcony. Elegant furnishings, silk wallpaper, stylishly expensive furniture. So this is how the 1 percent live.

Nice.

Hands on my waist divert my attention and Beck steps into my backside. My heart rate immediately accelerates, half of my body going into a defensive posture and the other half opening wide up to the slight possibility of something thrilling with this man. Sex is complicated for me. My first experience was so horrific I tried to kill myself after.

Since then, I've had good and bad.

Some men do nothing more than thrust, grunt, and unload. That's not so bad and it's over with quickly.

Some men are mediocre. They make attempts to get me off but are never successful, and I've become adept at faking the world's best orgasm, which strokes their ego nicely.

None have been fantastic. No one has ever made me go weak in the knees. Not one single man has ever inspired me to *want* to bring them to theirs.

Doesn't mean I haven't brought them to their knees, it just means that I've never found someone that I wanted to do that to.

No man has ever made me feel a connection to him past the

act of sex. My psychiatrist once told me that was because I had no emotional connection when I was raped. In fact, it was so cold, brutal, and without regard for me as a human being that I have a hard time understanding and accepting intimacy. I just can't reconcile that sex and kindness go together.

I've never in my life experienced an orgasm while having sex with a man. Had plenty with my vibrator, but a man has never gotten me off, and I don't need my psychiatrist to explain the reasoning behind that either.

To me, sex is just an act. I could do without it, but I also don't mind having it when it fits my agenda. In my past relationships, which have been few and far between, I had sex to make the other person feel good. More as a reward for treating me decently, and also maybe because while I may not have enjoyed it very much, it at least made me feel normal and not like a freak as I normally do.

Tonight, sex with Beck will further my agenda, so I'm all in.

Beck's hand lifts, pulls my hair away from my neck. I feel his lips press there softly and a shiver runs up my spine. My heartbeat increases in tempo and a rush of adrenaline flushes throughout me with dizzying repercussion.

Oh wow . . . that's new.

I suck in a deep breath and try to ground myself. His lips press harder against me, then I feel teeth against my skin. He scrapes them gently over me and a delicious ache forms between my legs.

That's also new, and the feeling is so disconcerting that I pull away from his embrace so I can get myself under control. My body has never reacted that way, and frankly, it scares the shit out of me, almost to the point that I consider running.

I cannot afford to lose control with this man, a prospect that is almost as terrifying as my memories of my sixteenth birthday.

Keep your eyes on the prize, Sela.

It's imperative that whatever happens tonight that I rock Beck North's world to such an extent that he wants to see me again. I need to keep my foot in the door and that means tonight . . . I cannot hold anything back. It has to be my best performance ever.

Turning to face Beck, I tilt my lips upward in a seductive curve and step into him. My hands go to his chest, slip upward and under his suit coat, to his shoulders where I push it off. It falls to the ground and before it hits, my hands are working his belt buckle.

It's a good thing too, because working the expensive, supple leather through the metal buckle helps to calm the shakiness of my hands. I pull the entire belt free and toss it away. My hands go immediately to the button of his dress slacks, but the minute I twist it free of the hole, Beck's hands are on mine . . . stilling my progress.

I look up slowly and Beck's eyes are sizzling with need. This gratifies me, because I know that I have what he wants and I have the power to hook him with it. I press against his hold and try to tug at his zipper, but he draws my hands away.

"Slow down a bit," he says gruffly as I look back up at him. "We have all night."

"All the more reason to let me give you a blow job right now," I tell him with sly look, and reach my hands out again. "Take the edge off."

"I like the edge," he says in a low growl. "I like getting worked up. I like waiting until it's even a bit painful. I also like being in charge, so those beautiful lips aren't getting anywhere near my cock right now."

Those words . . .

They both terrify and titillate me. And that ache between my legs starts to throb. I hate it because it's distracting me.

Beck North is totally throwing me off my game and we haven't even gotten naked yet.

CHAPTER 6

Beck

For a fleeting moment, I thought I saw fear on her face. It was so fast that I'm sure I imagined it. Almost like a strobe light . . . flashing bright and turning dark all within a microsecond.

It was when I told her that I needed to be in charge.

Sometimes fear is a good thing. It enhances the senses, ramps up the pleasure. But now I don't see it and I wonder if I imagined it, but regardless . . . I am now and will always be in charge of this woman tonight.

I'm not surprised by her aggressive moves, because since the minute I laid eyes on her she's done nothing but ooze self-confidence. And don't get me wrong, there is nothing wrong with a woman who wants to suck my dick in a forward fashion.

Just not tonight.

Tonight I want to show her that she doesn't have anything to show me that I haven't already seen before. Countless women have dropped to their knees and begged to deep throat me, all with the hopes that I'll never look at another piece of pussy again. I know Sela said she's not looking at me that way, and that she's actually talking to a Sugar Daddy, but I don't know her, which means I don't trust her. Trust doesn't come easy to me, because the people closest to me in life have done nothing but lie. And let's face it . . . trust isn't going to be formed tonight. Thus, I need to impress upon her the truth of my position.

She has nothing that I need.

The best way to show her that is to refuse instant sexual gratification. While it would be fucking phenomenal to have her suck me off, I need her to understand and truly believe me when I say I don't need it.

Best way to do that is to focus on her pleasure and not mine.

And that has never been a hardship for me, especially with one as beautiful and delectable looking as Sela Halstead.

"Let's get you out of this dress, shall we?" I step up to her, bring my hands around her back, and easily find the tiny zipper at midback. The minute I unzip her, the dress falls down in a swish of silver froth around her ankles. I take her by the hand and help her step free.

Her body is amazing and I take my time looking at it. Spectacular breasts that are heavy with pert nipples that are begging to spend some time between my teeth. Sleek and toned muscles, a flat stomach, and miles of smooth leg.

"Turn around," I murmur.

She does, and the tiny white lace thong is the perfect choice for her to wear, because her ass is spectacular. Her shoulders are graceful, her back arched perfectly as it flows into artful, sculpted glutes, and her thighs and ribbon-covered calves are ridiculously toned. This girl does some serious working out.

She continues her slow spin until she's facing me again. Her face is slightly flushed, but her eyes are challenging.

My hand goes to the knot of my tie and I work it loose. As I pull it over my head, I tell her with a nod toward the bedroom, "Go get on the bed."

Sela doesn't even argue, taking me at face value when I told her I was in charge. She turns and I'm treated to another great view of her luscious backside swaying back and forth as she walks into the suite bedroom.

I follow behind her, working at the buttons of my dress shirt. When I get the first three undone, I merely reach down and lift it along with the white T-shirt underneath over my head. They get dropped to the carpet.

When Sela reaches the bed, she bends to the side a bit, her fingers pulling on the silver ribbon that's tied from the heel of her sandals around her lower calf.

"Don't," I tell her, and she straightens to look at me over her shoulder. "Leave them on. They're sexy as fuck."

She nods and gives me a hint of a smile, turning to face me. I let my eyes glide down her body slowly, drinking in my fill of sheer perfection.

"You're stunning," I tell her truthfully, because words are good foreplay too.

Her eyes lower a bit, and I realize how long and thick her lashes are as they lay against the delicate, pale skin just underneath. I find that interesting that a little bit of praise and she turns shy. I'm betting this woman hasn't had a lot of men in her life tell her just how exquisite she is.

"I'm going to eat your pussy," I tell her bluntly, and her head snaps up, her eyes large and round with surprise. "So get your panties off and get in bed."

She hesitates for a moment and I see that flicker of fear again, and I have to wonder, why does that scare her? Is she afraid of losing control with me? God, I fucking hope so, because watching a woman like this losing it is going to be hot as hell.

Lifting her chin, Sela pushes her thong down those long legs and steps out of them. She turns and crawls onto the bed while I use the opportunity to pull a condom from my wallet and divest myself of my pants and underwear. I started getting hard when her dress dropped from her body in the other room, but fuck . . . as I turn to her now and see her lying on the bed with nothing but those silver high-heeled sandals with ribbon, my dick goes full-on salute out of respect for her beautiful body.

I toss the condom down onto the bed and look down at her. She holds my gaze, and the only sign of her discomfort is a slight reddening of her cheeks. It makes her not only beautiful, but with those bright blue eyes and freckles . . . it makes her look impossibly young, fresh, and naïve.

That makes me want to dirty her up a bit, so I push at her tender boundaries.

"Spread your legs, Sela," I command as I kneel on the bed. "Dig those spiked heels into the mattress and spread 'em wide."

A low bubble of anguish slips out of her mouth and I can't tell if it's because this is embarrassing her or is turning her on, but it's not of any real consequence. Once my mouth hits that pussy, she won't care one way or the other.

I bend over, placing my hands palm down on the mattress just below her ass. I lower my face and study the beauty of her before me. I love a woman who waxes, and to treat myself and her to a little touch, I run a single finger over the smooth, soft skin of her mound.

A strangled sound comes out of Sela but I don't look up at her. Instead I lower my head further, and with the tip of my tongue, gently prod at her clit.

The minute I make contact, Sela's hips shoot of the bed and I freeze when she says, "Don't."

My eyes raise up to meet hers, and she has a wild, feral look about her as she stares down her body at me, her heaving chest raised up by her elbows propped on the mattress.

Her breathing is labored and she licks at her lips. "I mean . . . I'm not sure . . ."

Even though I'm confused by it, I think I understand what's going on here. "Has a man never done this to you before?"

Her face now goes beet red and her eyes lower. Gone without a trace is the confident woman who walked into this suite with me, and she refuses to confirm or deny my theory.

Impossible, but I'm pretty sure this is all new to her.

How in the fuck has a woman this beautiful made it this far in life without a man gorging himself to death between those perfect legs?

I place my hand on Sela's chest and push her back down gently to the bed. I crawl up her body, pressing my weight down on her. My cock lays heavy against her pussy, but I do nothing but simply kiss her slowly.

She jerks in surprise, but her mouth immediately opens to me, and her hands curve around my neck. I let my tongue spiral with hers, prolonging the kiss until I can feel her relax underneath me.

When I pull my mouth from hers, she opens her eyes slowly and looks at me with confusion.

"Sela," I tell her, my voice rough with lust. "I swear it's going to feel good. It's going to be intense and it's okay for you to pull my hair, curse, or cry out. Fuck . . . please cry out and tell me how fucking good I'm making you feel, okay?"

She just blinks her eyes, almost in wonder.

"Trust me, Sela?"

She never responds, but I take her lack of refusal as a green light. I slide back down her body, never hesitating for a moment before putting my mouth back on her.

Her hips buck again and she lets out a guttural moan. While I let my tongue work slow, deliberate circles around her clit, she chants, "Fuck, fuck, fuck."

This makes me smile.

My tongue is right against her clit, and then I purse my lips and suck on it.

Sela's hands slap to my head, her fingers diving into my hair. She pulls in an attempt to remove me, and then just as quickly pushes my face into her. This tells me she's warring with herself. She likes the way this feels but is troubled by the dirty nature of having a man up close and personal with her most sacred place.

That fucking turns me on like nothing else, and I start moving my tongue faster.

"I can't," Sela moans as she gyrates her hips against me. "I can't. I can't."

Yes, she fucking can. I slide two fingers into her while I lash at her clit with my tongue, working it faster and faster. I can tell she's digging those spiked heels into the mattress hard because her hips push all the way off the bed.

"No, no, no, no," she murmurs to herself, even has she holds my face tight to her with an insane grip on my head.

Completely contradictory, her words having one meaning, her body another.

Perplexing and fascinating to me, it makes me burn with the need to make her orgasm. I pull my fingers free of her pussy, add a third, and push them back in deeply. I scrape my teeth on her clit then enclose my lips around it and I suck at her hard with intermittent smacks of my tongue against her.

"B-e-e-e-c-k," Sela cries out in one long, stuttering breath as her back arches off the bed and I feel her pussy clamp down on my fingers in a stranglehold while she starts to come. She holds that position for a few moments as I can feel the pleasure rippling through her, and then she flops back down to the mattress.

I look up her body at her, my tongue now drawing lazy patterns around her clit. I stay away from the sensitive button of flesh because I don't think she can handle it again so soon. Sela lifts her head up and stares back down at me.

Utter confusion.

Complete satiation.

Fear.

Acceptance.

Her head flops back down onto the bed and she lets out a shaky sigh. I pull my fingers free of her body, press a soft kiss on the bald mound of her pelvis, and inch my way back up her body. I hold my weight off of her, even though my cock is practically straining to push itself inside of her tight, wet heat.

Her face turns to the side as I hover over her. She chews at her lip in consternation.

"Sela," I say to get her attention. She turns those blue eyes my way and that lip pops free.

"That was your first time?" I ask her gently.

Her cheeks get red again and she tries to turn her face away. My hand comes out, holds her still. I bend down, give her a brush of my lips against hers, and say, "Hey . . . don't be embarrassed. I loved doing that to you. Plan on doing it again to you before the night is up."

She gasps, those eyes go rounder, so I lay it out to her as honestly as I can.

"Baby . . . your pussy is so goddamn sweet, I'm glad I was the first to take a bite of it—"

Sela starts shaking her head side to side adamantly. I cock an eyebrow at her. "What?"

"You weren't the first guy to . . . you know . . . kiss me there."

I tilt my head, not understanding where she's going with this. She takes in a quavering breath, lets it out slowly, and says, "That was the first time a man has made me have an orgasm."

My chin jerks inward with stunned surprise, and before my

brain can even fully process what that means, I swear to God my dick gets even bigger and harder. *It* knows what that means.

"You've never had an orgasm before?" I ask incredulously, and now my cock starts thumping with need to get inside her.

"I can give myself one," she clarifies.

"You've got to be shitting me," I mutter as I push up off her body and reach to the side to grab the condom. I tear the foil open and roll it onto my dick. My gaze goes back to her and she's watching me warily. "What type of fuckwads have you been with that didn't know how to pleasure you?"

She opens her mouth but I shake my head. "Never mind. Don't answer that. It will probably only piss me off."

Scooting my body and my rubber-clad dick right off the bottom of the bed until I'm kneeling on the carpet, I grasp Sela's legs and pull her down until her ass hits the edge of the mattress.

"What are you doing?" she gasps.

"Going to eat you out again . . . give you one more orgasm before I fuck you," I tell her simply before I latch my mouth down onto her again.

"No, I can't," she cries out, but again, those hands come back to my hair and she presses my face tighter to her.

Oh yes you fucking can, I think, and I wonder how many I can give her tonight.

CHAPTER 7

Sela

I lay absolutely still, contemplating my next move.

The sun rose about twenty minutes ago and I came fully awake, understanding that I was in Beck North's hotel bed.

He's on his back, one arm above his head on the pillow, the other resting across his lower stomach. He's utterly gorgeous lying there totally nude, as the covers and sheets got kicked to the carpet hours ago. His mouth is slightly parted while he sleeps, and I remember in vivid detail what those lips did to me last night.

I lift my head and take a moment for the unfettered access I have to look at his body. My prior sexual experiences have been hurried and mostly with my eyes closed. There was usually a lot of fumbling in between hot kisses before falling to the bed, so with my foreplay experience there wasn't a whole lot to see. Afterward, I never looked at my partner's body. Didn't have any interest, really, and I always covered myself up after the heat of passion cooled.

But Beck?

I'm totally dying of curiosity so I give in to it while he sleeps.

His body is perfect. He's well built but isn't overly muscular.

His skin is a tanned a light golden color. There's a smattering of dark brown hair on his chest, and another trail that starts from under his belly button and travels downward. He clearly takes care of himself, because the hair all around his penis is trimmed very short. Even though his hands are large and masculine, they are well manicured, and his hair looks rumpled perfectly . . . as if it were styled to look that great while still being a mess.

I look at his dick. I expect it might be overtired from last night. Right now it lays softly nestled in between his legs, still quite thick and long even in its rest.

I know exactly how thick and long it gets when it's swollen to capacity as he fucked me no less than three times last night, in between handing me out orgasms as if they were treats from an ice cream truck.

Gently, I lay my head back down on the pillow and consider that.

A man gave me an orgasm.

Multiple orgasms.

With his mouth, with his fingers. Once, just with the pounding of his cock within me. It's like once I started, my body was making up for years and years of having no sexual gratification.

That first one . . . oh God . . . it scared the shit out of me. I never knew anything could feel that good. Sure, I'd given myself the "O" before, but it was a mild quaking of pleasure that brought a soft smile to my face.

When Beck made me come that first time?

It was felt like the force of a nuclear explosion went off inside of me, and it shredded me from the inside out. It was so powerful that it rendered me nearly blind and deaf for a few moments. My brain was still trying to play catch-up with what it all meant before he pulled me to the end of the bed and put his mouth to me again.

The second time he made me come, tears leaked from my eyes from not only the joy of such perfect pleasure, but for the years wasted that I never felt such a thing before.

I have no clue why it happened and why he was the one to do it, but clearly Beck North simply doesn't have a problem pulling them from me. I'm not sure if he's magic or just so damned dedicated to the cause, but it was effortless on his part. I'm betting he could probably just look at me a certain way and I might explode.

My lips curve upward in a fulfilled smile, and for the first time I wonder if perhaps I'm not completely broken. I know I'm fucked up about a million different ways, but perhaps my ability to truly appreciate sex as something pleasurable was just lying dormant and wasn't completely obliterated when I was raped.

Turning my head on the pillow, I look back at Beck. I don't think either one of us expected to fall asleep, and I'm almost betting he's not the type who likes awkward conversation the next morning. If I were a kinder, gentler Sela Halstead, I'd do the guy a favor and slip out of bed quietly, then slip even more quietly out of his life.

But I'm not kind or gentle.

I am, however, thankful and I want to thank this man for what he helped me achieve.

I push up, straight to my knees, and inch down the bed. I have no hesitation when I take his softened penis in my hand and gently squeeze it. At first, I get no reaction, but when I squeeze it again, it starts to expand against my palm. Gently I start to stroke it, watching in fascination as it lengthens and the tiny wrinkles of the loose skin start to disappear as blood fills his shaft. I've never watched a man get hard before and it's fascinating.

"Sela," I hear Beck murmur, and I tilt my head to look at him.

His eyes are closed but there's a smile on his face. "What are you doing?"

I don't answer him.

I merely show him.

I bend over and take him into my mouth, straight back to my throat.

"Fuck," Beck groans, and he pushes the fingers of one hand into my hair and grasps the back of my head. "Feels good."

I moan my understanding and agreement against him, pulling up and down on his cock with hollowed cheeks and a swirling tongue. Beck, in turn, grunts and huffs out strangled sounds from deep in his throat. His fingers grip my hair but not hard, just enough to encourage my motions.

I'm relentless with him, bringing my free hand to his balls, which I gently roll between my fingers. My other hand follows my mouth up and down his cock, squeezing him in such a way that he curses and begs me to go faster.

So I do.

"Goddamn . . . Sela," Beck mutters as he punches his hips up. I take him deep and that impresses him. "Fuck that's good."

Up and down, up and down I go. Savoring his taste and the satiny texture of his skin against my tongue. I pause at the top and scrape my teeth over the tip before taking him down deep again.

"Oh fuck," he groans, and his hand pulls on my hair. "Pull off . . . I'm going to come."

Swallow it.

All of it.

My head spins from the unwanted memory as I suck hard on my way up, let him pop free of my mouth, and then I jack him vigorously.

One, two, three . . . four times and he starts jetting semen over my hand and onto his stomach. I continue to stroke him as I watch pleasure contort his face and the cords of muscle in his neck contract from the force of his orgasm. I stroke him softly as he starts to come down, and finally he hisses out a long breath of relief.

His eyes open and he looks at me. "That was amazing."

I give him a smile as I wipe my hand off on the sheet next to his hip. Shrugging, I merely say, "I wanted to do something nice for you."

Beck's brows furrow inward as he contemplates the return of a favor. "Did you enjoy doing that the way I enjoyed having my mouth between your legs last night?"

I refuse to blush and hold his eyes. "Yes. Very much."

And that's the truth. Up until the very end when past and present started to blur, what I liked most about that experience was in listening to Beck make all those sexy sounds. Knowing that I was responsible for so much pleasure was a turn-on itself.

"Then it's not a return of a favor," Beck says.

"What's not?" I ask, now lost in the conversation.

"You said you were doing me a favor. That would have bruised my ego badly if you only did that as a return gesture."

I nod in understanding. "Gotcha. I did that because I wanted to show you my appreciation, but I also very much enjoyed doing that to you."

Neither one of us mentions the fact that I didn't swallow and I wonder how important that is to him.

It's not something I ever do for men, having my first experience forced upon me, but for some reason I think I would with Beck. If he hadn't have pulled me off, I was so lost in the experience I might have swallowed, and I'm pretty sure I wouldn't have been wigged out about it.

"Listen," Beck says as he sits up, leaning his weight on one hand planted in the mattress. "I'm going to take a shower."

And, here it comes.

The brush-off.

He may not have kicked me out last night after our last round, but I suspect it's because he was too tired. But now Beck is reiterating the point he made to me last night and that I readily agreed to.

This was a one-night stand and nothing more would ever come of it.

I start to roll out of the bed, intent on finding my purse and my clothes, when he stops me dead. "Want to join me?"

Looking over my shoulder at him, I raise an eyebrow. "In the shower?"

"Well, yeah," he says with a smirk. "We'll shower, we'll fuck . . . then I'll even take you to breakfast."

I blink at him slowly, wondering what the hell is going on here. He's looking at me as if he doesn't want to let me go.

And for the first time since I left the party with Beck last night, I have an attack of conscience. From what I've read and observed so far, he's seemingly a good guy, and here I am using him. He showed me unbelievable pleasure last night, made me feel semi-normal as a woman, and apparently wants to take me out for pancakes.

It's not computing.

"Um . . . I need to check the messages on my phone, but I'll be there in a moment," I tell him, needing a few minutes to collect myself. I've got too many emotions swirling and competing for supremacy. I have got to get my head back on straight and remember why in the hell I'm even here.

I turn away from Beck and swing my legs out of the bed. I'm

not even self-conscious in my nakedness, merely walking out of the bedroom and into the main living area of the suite. Beck calls after me, "Will you grab me a bottle of water from the fridge?"

"Sure," I say over my shoulder, and I can hear him turn on the shower.

I walk to the mini-refrigerator that's part of a built-in liquor cabinet and pull out a bottle of water. What in the hell should I do?

Beck North wasn't on my radar yesterday. Now I've spent an unbelievable night with him, and he still has apparent interest in me. While I don't presume to think he's going to enter into a sugarship with me, I'm definitely not getting kicked out onto the street. Now I just have to figure out how to play this.

Walk out that door right now and be done with this? Figure some other way to get at JT, which will take longer, though?

Or do I try to hook Beck even further, draw him closer into my web, and use him to get in close enough to strike? No guarantee that will work. I mean, for all I know, he's going to fuck me again, buy me breakfast, and then cut me loose forever.

My fingers fiddle with the label of the bottle in my hands, contemplating which route I should take. Either one will still put me on a path to my goal. One will be easier, although I'll be sacrificing some of what few principles I have left to use Beck in that fashion.

The upside is more time with Beck. A little bit more time with a man who makes me feel like a real woman . . . whole, undamaged, and full of potential. That's a benefit I never would have expected, and I'm a little ashamed that it's something that I'm even considering as important.

But fuck it . . . I like how he made me feel last night.

Decision made, I ignore my pile of clothes on the floor and head back into the bedroom. I lay the bottle of water on the edge of the mattress and pad silently toward the bathroom. A billow of steam wafts out the door, and in the mirror over the large vanity I can see the naked form of Beck as he tilts his head back under the stream of water while one of his hands rubs a bar of soap over his chest. Then down his stomach and right in between his legs, where he glides it around the base of his cock, over his balls, and back up his stomach again.

God, that's so hot.

Then he turns around and I realize I'm going to get to look at his ass, something I haven't had the pleasure of yet. The minute he turns, I get just a peek of those tight twin globes paler than the rest of his tan skin, but then my breath catches as I look at his back. My hand reaches out, grabs hold of the doorjamb for balance, and I look at Beck with narrowed eyes.

On his right shoulder blade, taking up no more than five inches or so, a tattoo.

A red phoenix taking flight with wings and tail of flame.

Oh holy fuck.

Red bird on a rib cage.

Red bird on a wrist.

Red bird on a shoulder.

Red birds fucking everywhere, closing in on me.

A surge of terror mixed with adrenaline punches into my stomach and I spin from the doorway, stumble but catch myself, before running through the bedroom and out into the living area. I hastily put my dress on, abandoning my thong and heels, which are back in the bedroom. I can't even imagine how ludicrous I'll look walking through the lobby to hail a cab in early November with no shoes, but I can't give that another thought.

I have to get the fuck out of here.

With my heart pounding so hard I can hear it in my ears, I grab my purse from the table by the front door of the suite where I had left it last night and I leave, quietly shutting the door behind me.

I have no clue what that phoenix tattoo means, but I know one thing:

Right now, it scares the piss out of me.

CHAPTER 8

Beck

I hang up the phone with my attorney and lean back in my desk chair. His news is not good, but it's also not unexpected. I cannot force a buyout with JT unless he basically does something illegal regarding the business. And no . . . snorting coke in your office doesn't count. The language is clear and it means criminal acts specifically related to the operations of the business and that are detrimental to said business.

But as much as I am bothered by JT's behavior over the last several months, and it makes me extremely worried going forward, I certainly don't want to find that he's done something illegal. That just puts too much liability and risk on me, and I'd rather walk than face the potential of a criminal investigation brought on by a moronic and out-of-control partner.

So I need to either suck it up or break free.

The choice is easy right now . . . I'm going to have to suck it up and just ride his ass to stay focused. With us preparing to roll out the new Web platform that's in development, this could mean a 40 percent increase in revenue with virtually no increased overhead, which means a huge chunk of change. I don't own the proprietary rights to the coding—according to my lawyer—so if I walk right now, I'd be losing out on all of the gains when it launches next year.

So I'll hold tight and keep a careful eye on my partner.

I have to say, while the news from my lawyer wasn't good, it was a welcome relief from the multitude of insane thoughts that have been running through my head all day regarding my lovely and apparently skittish companion from the night before last. I'd been in the shower the following morning, soaping myself up, thinking of the way she worked my cock with her mouth. I got hard again and called out to her to hurry up. I got no response.

So I called out again.

Still nothing.

Curiosity got the better of me, so I turned the water off and got out of the shower. With a towel around my waist, I walked around the suite three times before I'd convinced myself she actually had left. It made no sense, especially because she left her shoes and panties. Panties I could understand, but leaving shoes behind in early November?

No way.

So she left in a hurry and I have to wonder what caused her to run.

Can't believe the prospect of a shower with me and breakfast would be scary.

Unless . . .

Unless she was totally serious about getting close to that Sugar Daddy in Santa Clara. Maybe she really just wanted a one-night stand and had her sights set elsewhere. And not that this guy would be a better catch than me, but considering I told her unequivocally that I didn't do relationships and not even to bother fantasizing about it, maybe that's exactly why she jetted out of the hotel without even a goodbye.

Honestly, I thought the Santa Clara Sugar Daddy was a bunch of bullshit she threw at me to cover for the fact she really was sniffing around me for a potential sugarship. But now I'm not so sure.

What complicates things even more is the fact that I gave her the first orgasm she ever had with a man. I can't even begin to describe what that felt like, knowing that I was responsible for bestowing that on her, and then being completely perplexed how a woman as beautiful as that went so long without finding a real man to pleasure her. Her past experiences must have been horrid, and just thinking that last night sent me into a mindless frenzy to make her come over and over again.

Sela called my name out many times and even cursed me when she said she couldn't give me one more. I then proved her wrong and accepted two more from her. It was the hottest night of my life, showing that beautiful woman all the joys of some really fantastic fucking. And I stayed purely vanilla with her too, and it makes me hard just thinking about some of the ways I could make her scream.

Fuck.

I have got to stop thinking about her.

It's over.

Done.

She left.

No way to find her.

Except . . . that's not true. I fucking created The Sugar Bowl website. If she's a Sugar Baby, with a few keystrokes I can access the database and have her house pinpointed in moments.

Drumming my fingers on my desk, I stare at my computer

screen and ponder the merits of doing just such a thing. I mean, what would be the purpose? Just to fuck her again?

That actually sounds like a fantastic reason.

Lurching forward in my seat, I grab my keyboard and pull it toward me. I navigate my way into the internal database of Sugar Babies, as of this month totaling over 1.6 million registered from all over the world. That's nothing compared to the almost five million registered Sugar Daddies who pay a flat thousand dollars to join, autorenewed each year. Do the math . . . you can figure out what that means. While our money comes from the Daddies, our current marketing efforts are aimed at trying to build up with more Babies. The bigger our pool of Babies, the more Daddies will join.

I type in *Sela Halstead*, and I'm surprised when actually three women come up by that name. I immediately rule out two of them, as they reside in Texas and Georgia. The third Sela Halstead has an Oakland address, so I choose that profile.

I'm immediately rewarded when a picture of her appears on my screen. Yes, that's the gorgeous woman I fucked my dick raw with the other night, but the picture doesn't do her justice.

My eyes scan her personal data, of which we don't require much.

She's twenty-six and I don't find that surprising. Her face is definitely more youthful with the freckles and wide, innocent eyes, but there's a wisdom there within their depths that tells me she's got a few more years under her belt than your average Baby. Enrolled at Golden Gate University and rents a small apartment in Oakland. It appears she works part-time at a diner to help fund her tuition. No criminal record. Not even a speeding ticket. She's the classic Sugar Baby.

I look at the Comm button and consider snooping further. The Comm button will lead me to the encrypted messages that

Babies and Daddies use to communicate. I'm not doing anything illegal, as our terms of service include all members' agreement that we are allowed to monitor activity to ensure no fraudulent or criminal activities are being carried out.

But do I really want to know just how far entrenched into a potential sugarship she's delved? Or should I just close out the screen and get the fuck back to work?

Images of Sela's back arched off the bed and the muscles in her pussy clamping down hard on my fingers the first time she came flash through my brain and I click on the button without another moment's hesitation.

Scanning through the messages, I can see several potential Daddies have reached out to her. She's responded to a few, but nothing more than a polite decline that she's not interested. And then I see a long history of exchanges dating almost two weeks back with a man in Santa Clara, California.

Frank Webert.

And fuck . . . lame-ass name aside, he's practically a perfect catch for her. He's on the younger side at age forty-two, reasonably fit and attractive, and made his money in robotics. That means he's super-fucking filthy rich.

I read the messages and he comes on strong with Sela. While there is no overt solicitation or request for sex, there's enough innuendo in his messages to her that he expects it. Her responses are flirtatiously vague but promising, and she did agree to meet with him this upcoming weekend.

My bet is that he'll have an agreement signed with her by Sunday.

I think about how that makes me feel.

I wonder if he can make her come the way I did.

I wonder if she'll suck his cock like—

Surging up out of my chair, I grab my keys and phone off my

desk. I look at her home address one more time and commit it to memory before logging off my computer.

I walk out of my office and tell Linda in passing, "I'm going to be out for the rest of the day. I'll return calls tomorrow."

"No problem," she says with an affectionate smile. "Need me to do anything while you're gone?"

I stop and look back at her, wondering if I've gone temporarily insane. "Yeah . . . as a matter of fact . . . print me out a blank sugar agreement."

Linda blinks at me in surprise, momentarily stunned to inaction. I raise my eyebrows and lift my chin toward the printer that sits on the corner of her desk. She immediately jumps to it, taps her fingers on her keyboard a few times, and then the printer starts spitting out the document.

She pulls it off, staples the two pages together, and hands it to me with wide eyes. "Are you going to sign that?"

"I have no clue what I'm fucking doing," I mutter as I walk down the hall toward the main door.

I check my watch for about the twentieth time and glance down Nineteenth Street. No sign of Sela yet.

I've been parked outside her Oakland apartment at the corner of Twelfth and Nineteenth, not sure what direction she'd be coming from. I'm taking a guess she's using BART to get to and from school, so I expect to see her walking down Nineteenth from the train station. It's all supposition, and for all I know she's got a car that gets her back and forth, but I doubt it. That's a chunk of change to pay for gas and parking over at Golden Gate, and if she's in the market for a Sugar Daddy I'm guessing she's a BART girl.

It's nearing five P.M., starting to get dark, and I'm about ready to give up for the day. I've been sitting in my car nearly two hours and my ass is numb. I'm also starving, as I haven't eaten since breakfast. I can always try again tomorrow. Or hell, maybe I should just call her. I have her phone number from the database.

Just as my hand reaches for the ignition, I see Sela heading straight toward me. The sidewalk isn't overly crowded, although there are several people walking in both directions, but regardless . . . I recognize her immediately. I spent so much time touching and licking that body, I'd recognize it anywhere.

She's dressed a far cry from her sexy dress of last night. Today she's got on faded jeans that are ripped in one knee, black Converse tennis shoes, and a faded Raiders sweatshirt to ward off the chill. Her hair is pulled back into a ponytail and she has a heavy-looking backpack slung over her right shoulder as she trudges toward her apartment building.

I hop out of my car and lock it, hoping it will remain safe enough in this neighborhood. While it's not the worst, it's certainly not the best, and I've heard Audis are popular cars to boost.

Heading toward the front door of the building, I lengthen my stride and make it there about a second before she does. I grab the door, open it, and her head raises up as she says, "Thanks."

Her eyes flare large with worried surprise and she takes a step back from me. "What are you doing here?"

My hand shoots out and pulls the backpack from her shoulder, and fuck . . . that's heavy. "Came to see you. You left without saying goodbye."

"Wasn't any need," she says smoothly. "It was a one-night stand, right?"

"That's right," I say with an agreeable smile. "But I have to say, you had me worried when you left without even bothering to get your shoes. That tells me you were running, and I want to know why."

For a moment, I think she might tell me to go to hell, but her shoulders sag. With a small sigh, she steps past me into her building and says over her shoulder, "Might as well come up and we can talk about it."

Now that surprises me. I figured I'd have a bit more of a fight on my hands, but I graciously take the offer and follow her inside.

CHAPTER 9

Sela

Yes. Without a doubt . . . the red phoenix on the back of Beck's shoulder freaked me out when I first saw it. It was almost a slap in the face after what we'd shared just hours before.

After what he commanded my body to do.

So I ran without my panties or shoes, luckily caught a cab waiting right outside the hotel lobby, and didn't have a nosy cab driver asking me where my shoes were.

I tossed and turned all night, but by the time the sun rose, I think I had reasoned out some acceptance in my head.

First, I have no clue what that fucking tattoo means. As sinister as my rapists were, at first I thought it could be a cultlike symbol among sick fucks that like to rape together. I Googled it relentlessly six months ago when I first saw JT on the TV and realized that tattoo was very real and not just a nightmarish figment of my imagination. I researched it thoroughly and didn't come up with a damn thing. Whatever the reason behind that tattoo, it's not been publicized in any way.

Second, I have to consider that the tattoo could be something as innocuous as a fraternity thing. In fact, that's the most obvious answer, and since Beck and JT went to the same college and were friends even prior to that, it stands to reason that perhaps they were in a fraternity together. Or shit . . . maybe they were on some type of coed sports team that had matching tattoos. Who knows why guys do stupid shit like that?

Third, and probably most important, what I reasoned out was that just because Beck had a tattoo that matched my rapist didn't mean that he was by association a rapist. I have absolutely no recollection of him being there that night, although I'm the first to admit the Rohypnol I was given has fucked with my memories. I'm relying on nothing more than a deep, internal gut instinct about that. I just don't get that vibe from Beck. Sure, I could be very wrong about this. I could have piss-poor judgment, and perhaps I'm still riding high on the never-ending orgasms of last night, but I just don't think he has that in him. He seems like a decent guy, although I do question his choice of business partner who is evil incarnate.

Regardless, by the time I got out of bed this morning, I figured I'd made a crucial mistake by leaving Beck in the shower. It was a missed opportunity on my part to try to keep his interest in me piqued. He was my best chance at getting close to Townsend, and in a burst of emotional panic, I'd messed that up, which meant that I'd have to start all over again in my planning.

But now, Beck is here and I've been given a second chance to latch on to opportunity.

He follows me into my small apartment, carrying my backpack for me like a gentleman. I mean, the mere fact he looked up my information and drove here because he was worried seems to lend credence to my gut instinct that he's a decent guy. Of course, if he is, then I'm a supreme bitch for wanting to use him for my own agenda, but I never claimed to be a saint.

I do, however, have to be careful here, because I can't let my own personal feelings of affinity for him deter me from my path. I've got too much rage invested in my plan for retribution, and if I don't see this through, I'm afraid the failure will destroy me.

"Want something to drink?" I ask him as I walk into the kitchen. I open the fridge and do a quick perusal. "I have beer or milk that's probably spoiled. The tap water is decent though."

"I'm good," he says, so I close the door and turn to face him.

God, he looks good. He's casually dressed in a pair of dark jeans, brown loafers, and a blue-checked button-down. His hair styled, of course, in full *GQ* mode, and just a hint of stubble that suggests he didn't shave this morning.

"So why did you run?" he asks me bluntly, his face placid with only a hint of worry showing. I have a feeling this man is very good at schooling his emotions.

I certainly can't say, *Well, your red tattoo freaked me out and I thought for a brief moment you could be a rapist.*

But I am a quick thinker and I go with an answer that has a tiny hint of truth in it. "I was a little overwhelmed by everything that happened between us. It was . . . um . . . intense. I panicked, I guess."

Beck tilts his head and his brows draw inward as if that's not quite sitting right with him. He takes a step toward me across the faded linoleum, reaches a hand out, and tucks the tips of his fingers in the waistband of my jeans. With a tiny tug, he pulls me forward so I'm just a foot away from him. His voice is low, husky . . . shiver-inducing. "You mean that I handed you your first orgasm from a man?"

"And multiple ones at that," I whisper back, feeling hypnotized by the intensity of his stare.

"You shouldn't have run. I had more to give you." He tugs again on my waistband and I step into him close enough that my breasts brush against his lower chest.

"My bad," I say, a wave of disappointment washing through me that I may never have that again.

Beck stares down at me and I get the feeling he wants to kiss me, but I can't be sure. I've never been savvy or in tune with notions of romance and seduction. Guys want to fuck me, they usually just tell me that straight up.

With his free hand, Beck pulls something from his back pocket, then he's raising it between our bodies, causing me to take a step back. His fingers stay lodged in my waistband, so I don't go far. He waves a document in front of me that is stapled and folded in half lengthwise.

My eyes go from the paper to him. "What's that?"

"A sugar agreement," he says.

A flush of excitement causes my skin to prickle, but I'm still not sure what he means. "For who?"

"You and me," he says somberly, and possibly with even a slight grimace. He clearly doesn't want to do this, and yet . . . here he is offering it.

I step back, dislodging his hand from my jeans and cross my arms. With a skeptical cock of my brow, I state, "You're not a Sugar Daddy."

"That's true."

"And you told me unequivocally that you don't want to devote your time or resources to just one woman."

"Also true."

"Then why are you here in my apartment with an agreement?" I ask in exasperation.

"Because you need a Daddy to fund your schooling and I'm feeling generous," he says slyly, and I know that has nothing to do with why he's standing here.

"I have someone that's already interested in that. In fact, I plan to seal the deal this weekend," I counter.

I truly don't have any intentions of signing an agreement with the very rich and slightly pushy Frank Webert. That conversation was begun merely to maintain my cover as a naïve Sugar Baby on the prowl . . . nothing more.

And by the tight look on Beck's face, I'm guessing he doesn't like that at all.

"I can give you something he can't," Beck says confidently as he sets the agreement on my kitchen table.

"Oh yeah . . . what's that?" I ask almost breathlessly, but I know damn well what he can give me.

Beck steps back into me, backs me right up against my refrigerator, and pulls my jeans open with efficient and practiced fingers. I gasp as his hand slips down my panties and his fingers drag against me slowly.

"How about I show you," he murmurs, in an almost taunting tone.

But I don't care.

I'm immediately gone.

I can tell by the easy glide of him against me that I'm soaking wet. I'm wondering at what point that occurred.

When he told me he can give me something no other man can?

When he showed me the agreement?

Hell . . . probably when he opened the door for me downstairs.

Regardless, my body reacts to Beck in a way that's totally contrary to my entire being. Since that night when my innocence and part of my sanity was taken, I've never let anyone get to me the way Beck has. I've always been able to keep emotion separate from sex, but for whatever reason, my body just doesn't want to behave when he's in close proximity.

The tip of Beck's finger circles slowly around my clit and he places a hand on the refrigerator next to my head. Tilting his own, he leans in and presses his lips to my jaw. Slides over and whispers in my ear, "How fast are you going to come for me, Sela?"

I moan in response, my blood racing, and my heart about ready to leap out of my chest.

"I'm betting pretty fast," he says with a husky laugh. "Just look at the way your hips are moving . . . trying to ride my finger."

I don't have to look. I can't seem to stop myself.

Pressure builds, there's that telltale tightening in my lower back, an almost frustrated cramp of pleasure between my legs, then Beck presses down on my clit, and I explode. My body pushes off the refrigerator, pressing into him hard while my head falls back. A long moan tears free of my throat, and I realize my fingers are dug deep into his biceps. I'm not even sure when that happened, but I have to consciously flex my fingers to let him go.

As I open bleary eyes, I see him looking down at me in triumph. He pulls his hands from my pants, sticks his finger in his mouth, and sucks it with relish. "Delicious," he says with a twinkle in his eyes.

"Damn, you're really good," I say as I suck oxygen back into my lungs.

"So sign the agreement," he says nonchalantly. "I'll do that to you quite frequently."

"And what's in it for you?" I ask suspiciously, because I can't believe he's gone from adamant bachelor to offering a commitment.

And yes . . . a sugarship is a commitment . . . at least monetarily.

Beck steps away from me and I use the opportunity to fasten my jeans. He turns, grabs the agreement, and hands it to me. "I'm fascinated by you," he tells me bluntly. "There's an innocence about you. The fact that I can give you something that no other man has . . . well, let's just say that does nice things to my ego."

"This is an ego trip for you?" I ask, astounded.

"Partly," he says without an ounce of shame. "And partly because I'm attracted to you on a level that I've not previously experienced. That says something, right?"

"And other than orgasms, what do I get?"

He waves the document at me and I take it. Unfolding it, I skim through the standard language and flip to the second page where it's typed:

Sugar Daddy hereby agrees to:

And written in blue ink in a messy scrawl that I assume is Beck's script:

> Pay for Sela Halstead's master's degree at Golden Gate University, which includes, but is not limited to, tuition, books, and housing, as well as a stipend to cover wages she would earn at any jobs she currently holds. Sugar Daddy will also pay off any existing school loans, both undergraduate and graduate, taken out by Sela Halstead to date.

My head snaps up and my mouth hangs wide open. "You're paying for my entire education?"

He shrugs and shoves his hands into his pockets. "It's what I'd pay for a vacation for myself. No biggie."

"No biggie" my ass, and he's also full of shit when he says he'd pay that much for a vacation for himself. Beckett North isn't flashy like that. While having my degrees paid for was never, ever a consideration when I decided to become a Sugar Baby to pursue Townsend, the mere thought of having that debt off of me almost makes me light-headed. It's almost too good to be true.

My eyes narrow at the agreement. "And what do I have to do?"

But he doesn't answer, instead letting me read the next paragraph outlining my obligations. Again, in his handwriting, I will agree to:

> Move in to Beck North's home for a period of one month. Quit all jobs currently employed at. Outside of school conflicts, attend any and all functions with Beck North and appropriate attire will be provided.

And that's it.

Nothing else.

Very short, simple requirements handwritten by Beck.

My head raises slowly and I'm almost disappointed when I say, "You want me to move into your house for one month and just be your date to various functions?"

Beck gives a dark laugh, pulls a pen from his breast pocket, and hands it to me. "No, Sela. I expect you to also be in my bed each night, which is why I don't want you working at some diner, and that you'll let me fuck you in any way that I want. But of course that can't be put into the agreement."

My knees almost buckle. The way he just said he wants me to let him fuck me any way he wants is almost menacing, and to someone with my issues, a little terrifying. Yet my knees almost buckle, mostly from the prospect of immense pleasure I think will come with that.

I stare at him a moment and my eyes flip to the pen he's holding out. I don't hesitate before grabbing it. I turn, spread the document on the counter, and hastily scrawl my name on the bottom. Beck takes the pen, adds his name under mine, and the deal is sealed.

I lift my face, wondering if he'll add a kiss onto the agreement, but instead I find him looking at me with determination. "Sela . . . it's just a month. Nothing long-term."

"I understand," I say, and think, *That should be more than enough time to figure out a better, more secure plan to go after Townsend.*

Finally, he gives me a smile and leans in, brushing his lips against mine. "Then let's get your stuff packed up. You're moving in tonight."

CHAPTER 10

Beck

I unlock the door to my apartment, anticipating seeing Sela. She's been here for a week in my penthouse condo in the Millennium Tower, and I'm still surprised when I come home from work and find her here. It's not that it's hard to get used to sharing my space with another person; it's that she's made it so fucking easy, and that's what has shocked me.

I honestly figured I'd see a little play once she moved in. I would only commit to a month, figuring I'd get sick of the arrangement, because, let's face it . . . how fucking enamored can I actually be with her? I mean, yeah . . . when she comes whether it's on my tongue, my fingers, or my cock, it's like the most miraculous thing I've ever seen. It takes over her entire being . . . it transforms her from an aloof, beautiful creature to one who, just for a few moments, seems to open up part of her soul. It's practically spellbinding.

At any rate, maybe she figures she's got me dazzled, because the play I expected never occurred. I've heard enough from JT and some other Sugar Daddies that when you take on a Sugar

Baby, you are given some pretty spectacular royal treatment. That first night I came home, I half expected her to meet me at the door with some sexy lingerie on and a casserole in the oven. I expected her to drop to her knees and give me the best fucking blow job ever.

You know . . . so she could show me that she deserved to be here longer than a month.

Instead, I found her on the couch studying, her forehead scrunched while she chewed on the eraser of a pencil. She raised her head, gave me a half smile, and said, “Hey,” before returning to her textbook.

And that was it.

I’ll admit . . . a small part of me was disappointed, because who wouldn’t want a blow job as soon as you walked in the door? But most of me respected her for it, because she was clearly showing me that she was more than just a fuck.

Didn’t mean I didn’t fuck her though.

In fact, I immediately walked over to the couch, pulled the book from her hand, and hauled her up. Just in case she thought to fight or deny me, I bent over and pushed my shoulder into her stomach before putting her into a fireman’s carry. And, music to my ears, I think I even heard a tiny laugh.

Because I didn’t fuck her that first night she moved in, I was a little impatient in my need and I bypassed heavy foreplay, doing just enough with my fingers and dirty words to get her wet. I fucked her hard, intent on getting her off with the power of my cock alone, and it was beautiful when she came, especially when my name came out in a ragged cry of relief and gratitude.

I’m wondering tonight what I’ll get with Sela. Most nights, she’s been on the couch studying. One night she didn’t even come home until almost ten P.M., claiming a study session at the library. On another night, I walked in to the smell of baking lasagna and a naked Sela in my bed waiting for me. She had the sheet resting over her breasts and she looked unsure of herself, but she gamely invited me to come play with her. Her idea of playing was to ride me slowly until my brain almost exploded and my dick very nearly did when I came.

Setting my keys down on the small side table near the door, I traverse the dark hardwood flooring in the hall to the massive open-plan living room that's bordered on two sides by floor-to-ceiling windows that overlook Oakland Bay, with the Bay Bridge and Oakland hills in the distance. Sela's not in the living room studying, but I know she's here because her ratty backpack is on the floor beside the couch.

I move to the hall that leads to the other side of the condo, which takes up the entire top floor of my building. The bedroom areas are separated from the openness of the living, kitchen, and dining areas, with the master bedroom at the end of the hall. Normally, as soon as I step into the bedroom, my attention is always taken by the same floor-to-ceiling windows that overlook the Financial District and Coit Tower, but instead I'm drawn to Sela sitting on my carpeted floor with a pile of my clothes all around her. She's currently folding a white T-shirt of mine into a crisp, neat square and setting it carefully in a drawer.

"What are you doing?" I ask, watching her with a mix of amazement and confusion.

"Organizing your drawers and straightening up your clothes," she says without even looking at me. "I'm guessing you just dump your clothes in whatever drawers are easiest to reach right from the dryer."

Her voice holds a hint of an amused laugh, but I still can't tell because her back is to me. I shed my suit jacket, as I had to dress up for some meetings, and work my tie loose. I move to the end of the bed and sit down, which now lets me see the side of her face . . . the graceful curve of her neck . . . the freckles across her nose and cheek.

And fuck . . . when did freckles start to get me hard?

"You don't have to do that for me," I tell her as she pulls another wrinkled white T-shirt from the pile beside her and starts to fold it.

She shrugs. "I don't mind."

I lean forward, snag her wrist, and tug at her. "But I do."

Sela turns her beautiful head my way and grins at me. "You're a total slob to live with, so while I'm here, expect me to do a little cleaning and organizing. Besides, I'm tired of living out of my suitcase and want a little room of my own."

I pull on her harder and she comes up to her knees while dropping the shirt from her hand, and when I continue to pull, she finally comes to her feet. I bring my hands to her waist, lean back, and pull her down on top of me as I lay back against the mattress. She falls onto my body, her hands going to my chest and her long hair falling forward to shield us.

"Seriously," I say with our noses almost touching. "You do not have to clean this place. Or organize me. Or do anything for me at all."

The smile slides from her face a bit and she murmurs, "But I do *have* to do something for you, right? You are my Sugar Daddy, after all."

I grimace and bring a hand to her face, gripping her chin. "Don't call me that."

She blinks in surprise at the vehemence in my voice. Tilting her head, she asks, "You don't like your own business very much, do you?"

I'm now the one that blinks at her in surprise. "On the contrary, I like my business very much. We provide a great service to both the men and the women who have joined."

"Then why don't you want to be called a Sugar Daddy?" she asks.

I roll our bodies over, putting her flat on her back and coming to rest on top of her. I press my elbows into the mattress and stare down at her. "I had you sign that ridiculous agreement to get you here with no arguments. But I wouldn't hold you to it. I have you here because I find you fascinating and I'm very much enjoying fucking you. That's all there is to it."

"But the money you paid—"

"It's yours no matter what happens," I tell her, and that's true enough. I had her give me a summary of all related expenses for the year she's already taken of the course and the one she's now finishing up, as well as the information on her undergraduate loans, and I deposited those funds into her bank account. It's an amount that's paltry in comparison to my fortune, and I won't miss it a bit.

Her eyes go warm and sad all at once. "I feel like I'm taking advantage of you. You pay for my college and give me amazing orgasms, and I can leave whenever I want. I just don't get it."

"I'm just fucking magnanimous that way," I tell her with a grin, and then press my lips to hers. She laughs, which causes her mouth to open, and I slide my tongue in.

We kiss for a moment, but my cock seems to think that's an open invitation to come play, so I pull my mouth from hers and push up off of her. Rolling to the side, I stand up and hold my hand out to her. "Come on . . . let's go eat at The Slanted Door. We'll gorge on oysters and ceviche."

She places her hand in mine and lets me pull her from the bed. She looks absolutely amazing in jeans and a T-shirt, no makeup on her face. I imagine most Sugar Babies walk around with perfect makeup and hair along with whatever designer clothing their Daddies decide to buy for them. The only thing that Sela's asked for since we moved in was a tea kettle, since she prefers tea to coffee.

"I'm going to finish putting these clothes away," she says as she releases my hand and starts to kneel back down on the carpet. And then as an afterthought, she asks, "I was dust mopping the condo today but the middle bedroom is locked. Want me to clean in there?"

I roll my eyes and start to pull my tie from around my neck. "No, Cinderella . . . I don't want you to clean that room."

"What's in there?" she asks as she folds another T-shirt. "Some top-secret stuff?"

I laugh as I turn to look at her, pulling the tie free. "It's my office."

I expect her to laugh with amusement and ask why the door is locked, which wouldn't bother me in the slightest. I do have some proprietary information in there like my financial records and copies of my business agreements. Stuff that's nobody's business but my own, and before Sela moved in, I made sure to lock that door.

Yes, I expect but her to laugh and joke about the locked door, but instead, I see something cloud her eyes. Consternation, maybe? Calculation?

I'm not sure, and she turns her face from me to the next T-shirt, so I can't continue to analyze it.

But then Sela says, "Want a blow job before we go to dinner?" and I'm completely thrown off track. Whatever look was on her face is completely forgotten.

She turns her face to me, blue eyes round and innocent with just a hint of mischief in their depths.

I start to unbutton my shirt as I look at her sitting on my floor with one of my tees in her hand. "Why do I get the feeling you're redirecting me?"

She shrugs and gives me a tiny smirk. "I just wanted to return to the notion of you telling me that you don't expect anything, because that's not exactly true. You do expect to have sex with me, and I'm just reminding you of that. I'm just throwing in the cleaning out of the goodness of my heart."

My fingers freeze on the buttons as I consider what she's said, and I realize that while I very much would enjoy the fuck out of a blow job from her, she's completely wrong about why she's here in my condo. She's not here so I can have available pussy 24/7 without having to work for it. And she's not here for my pleasure or whim. That's all easy stuff for me to get.

I brought Sela Halstead to my home for one reason only, and that's because that first night we were together, with my lips sucking on her clit and I was three fingers deep inside of her, something happened when she came that changed the course of her life and mine. I can't explain it, and perhaps it is nothing more than an ego trip for me like I told her a few nights ago. But I do know one thing for sure . . . there is some type of connection between Sela and me that I've never experienced before, and frankly, I'm just fucking curious about it.

Whatever the connection . . . for whatever reason that I've given her something that others haven't, I have a deep gut instinct that it's something that defies reason or logic. I almost get the sense it's mystical in nature, and I'm intrigued beyond measure. And so for the first time in my life, I'm doing something that is completely unlike anything Beck North has ever done before.

I'm exploring something deeper with one woman.

This woman to be exact.

CHAPTER 11

Sela

Moving in with Beck was a bit disorienting at first.

New home.

New bed.

New sex life.

Sex every night, usually multiple times.

Orgasm after orgasm, Beck not once having failed to deliver. It's almost effortless for him, and even I can't bring myself to such quick and dizzying heights as he's able to.

For the first few days, it was easy to give in to it. I'd go to my classes and then come back to his place. He gave me a key and told me to make myself comfortable, and thus I did. I treated his home like my own, and kept my schedule the same, outside of giving up my job at the diner. Beck's "stipend" to compensate for that was so generous, and given that my school expenses were paid, I wouldn't have to work again until after I got my degree, and hopefully never again in a diner. So in my downtime, I studied even harder, and the only deviation was when Beck commanded my attention. It was ridiculously easy for him to do so.

But after a few days, I settled in and started to think again of my plot to avenge myself. Beck and I haven't necessarily talked a lot. I don't get the feeling he's closed off, it's just that neither one of us has made much of an effort to get to know the other person outside of the best way to pleasure each other. For him, I think that's because he's focused on sex. For me, it's because I need to remain aloof . . . detached. It's the best way to keep my heart protected.

But on the sex front, we know quite a lot about each other, and I figure the more he's distracted with sex, the less chance he'll ever have of figuring out the woman behind the façade.

After I had been here four days, I decided I needed to get my bearings and figure out if there was anything about my current arrangement that was going to help me murder Jonathon Townsend. I searched Beck's home top to bottom one afternoon after my classes got out. It was pristine, almost sterile, and in a fit of anxiety over not finding anything, I dumped out all of his clothes from his drawers to make sure I didn't miss something. That, of course, led me to an impromptu lie when he came home and found me sitting amid all of his clothing.

But if I'm only here for a month, the clock is ticking, and I'm closing in quickly on the halfway mark. I've got to get closer to Beck and figure out more about his relationship with JT. Only then will I be able to determine if there is a way he can unwittingly help me achieve justice.

The only potential I've seen so far is his locked office. I've searched high and low for a key, and the only one I've been able to identify is the one that Beck keeps on his key chain with his car and house keys. He's used it twice since I've been here, merely going in after work and placing some documents he brought home in there. He always has those keys in his pocket when he's out and about, but when he comes home he places them on the side table by the foyer door. I haven't quite figured out how to get in his office, but I'm mulling it over.

And while my ultimate goal is to use Beck to my advantage in my quest, there is a more pressing goal that came to my attention just last night. Beck had gotten to the condo around six P.M., which was usually standard. As normal, he had his mail that he'd picked up in his hand, flipping through it. I was sitting at his dining table, which sat perpendicular to the length of the open living room and afforded a gorgeous view of the bay at sunset.

He'd started a habit of walking over to me and kissing me on the top of my head. The first time he did it, I was taken aback. It had been so long since I'd been shown a spontaneous act of affection I wasn't sure I liked it. But the next night he did it, it felt nice. And the night after that, even better.

It had gotten to where I expected it now, and it was a silly ritual that brought me a measure of almost schoolgirl giddiness, something I don't think I ever experienced since my interest in high school boys was killed that night ten years ago. I avoided them like the plague thereafter and didn't even kiss another man until I was twenty years old and quite drunk.

So Beck walked over to me at the dining room table and plopped the mail down by my books. He kissed me on the top of my head, and then grabbed my ponytail, tugging on it so my face tilted. He kissed me from above, this time on my mouth, and murmured, "Hey, gorgeous."

"Hey," I whispered back.

"What do you feel like for dinner?" he asked, releasing my hair and pulling his jacket off.

"I'm not picky," I said. "And I'm done studying."

"Let's do something casual," he said, and started walking back toward his bedroom. My eyes dropped to the pile of mail, and I saw an envelope that he had already opened with what was clearly a birthday card sitting on top of it. My hand reached out, never once considering his privacy, and I picked up the card. It was generic-looking with a birthday cake on the front. On the inside just a simple printed message, HAPPY BIRTHDAY.

Under that it wasn't even signed, but was stamped in calligraphy with the names MR. AND MRS. BECKETT NORTH, SR.

His parents.

A rush of anger and sadness hit me all at once, that this was the type of card they would send their son. I got up from my chair and walked into Beck's bedroom. He'd already shed his work clothes and was pulling on a pair of jeans. He looked up at me with a smile, then his eyes dropped to the card in my hand, back up to me with the same smile.

"Today's your birthday?" I asked quietly.

He laughed and nodded at the card in my hand. "Actually it was two days ago. My mom's secretary is apparently late in sending that to me."

I gasped in outrage. His parents actually had someone send a card to him? And it was late on top of that?

Beck buttoned his fly and walked up to me, taking my face in my hands. He looked at me with sympathy.

Me.

With sympathy.

"Relax, Sela," he said with a laugh and then a kiss to my lips. "That's par for the course. I didn't expect anything different."

And while that made me feel marginally better, I still felt terrible. "But I was here two days ago with you. We went out to eat at The Slanted Door. You gorged on oysters and ceviche, and never once did you tell me it was your birthday."

"It's just a birthday," he told me as he wrapped his arms around me. He kissed me again on top of my head, a measure of reassurance and affection that I'm upset on his behalf, and this act caused my stone heart to start to crack.

Beck then started talking about a new restaurant he wanted to try that had opened a few blocks over from the condo, and the subject of his birthday was put to rest.

Until today, that is.

I woke up with a plan already formed. I went to my classes, and as soon as they let out at one P.M., I hustled to the local market. I bought some beautiful salmon steaks, fresh asparagus, and a chocolate-raspberry cake from the bakery. I had thought briefly to bake him a cake, but I suck at baking and am only mediocre at cooking, so in order to preserve the sanctity of the only birthday party he was getting this year, I went with items that I couldn't screw up. I also bought a large roll of silk floral ribbon in a pale pink color.

I did my studying, took a shower, slathered lotion all over me, and curled my hair. I applied a little bit of makeup and brushed my teeth. Wearing one of Beck's robes, I managed to get the salmon steaks and asparagus in the oven, let them cook the required time, and then turned the heat off. It was ten of six when I scurried back to the bedroom and ditched the robe, picking up the silk ribbon.

And now at six P.M. I am lying in wait in the foyer when I hear Beck's key in the lock.

I quickly light the candles on the cake I'm holding in one hand and then toss the lighter onto the nearby buffet table. I have just enough time to place my free hand on my hip and cock it out in a sexy pose when Beck opens the door.

I wish I had a video to capture the look on his face. His eyes go to the cake first, then to my face as I smile at him and say, "Happy birthday, Beck."

His lips curve up and his eyes roam over my body, turning hotter and hotter with every inch they cover.

"Are you my present?" he asks in a husky voice as his eyes light back on mine. He closes the door behind him softly and flicks the lock.

I look down at myself, once again impressed with my ingenuity. I'm completely naked except for two things. The high-heeled silver sandals with ribbons that lace up my legs that Beck had returned to me, and pink silk ribbon wrapped from the very top of my thighs, around my ass and pelvis, covering my stomach, and on upward to wrap around my breasts. I finished the wrapping off with a bow right in the center of my chest.

"Come blow out your candles and you can unwrap me," I whisper.

What I'm doing right now is a monumental feat for me. It's the only time in my entire life I've ever made a conscious effort to seduce a man. I have never once offered myself up in such a sexy and overt manner. Two days ago when I waited in Beck's bed naked doesn't count, because that was my terrible attempt to be a good Sugar Baby, and it was completely lame. I did it because I felt I owed him for paying for college, and no other reason. I did it because I thought he was expecting it.

Tonight is different though.

I am doing this for Beck because I *want* to do this for him. I want him to have a memorable birthday because the one he had three days ago was shitty. And I want to see him smile because of it and know that someone on this earth is thinking about him in the way that he deserves.

"You are too much," he murmurs as he drops his keys on the side table and prowls toward me.

He stops just inches away, the light from the candles making his face glow and his eyes to sizzle. I give him an impertinent smirk. "I only put five candles on. Didn't want to burn down the house, old man."

Beck snickers and turns to blow out the candles. "I'm only twenty-eight and I'm going to make you pay for that 'old man' comment."

Beck takes the cake from my hand and turns to set it on the table beside his keys. As he turns back to me, he eyes the bottom of the ribbon hugging my thighs. "Got anything on under that pretty bow?"

"Nope," I tell him, my hand still resting on my hip and trying to hold my sexy pose. I have no clue if I'm pulling it off, but Beck seems to appreciate what he sees.

"Perfect," Beck murmurs, and his hands come to my shoulders. He turns me around and starts pushing me toward the dining room table. He kicks one of the massive chairs covered in cream leather to the side and uses an arm to push my books away, clearing a space just in front of me.

"Bend over," he says as he puts a hand to the center of my back and starts pushing me forward.

Immediately I flush all over with warmth and awareness of what this must look like. I know the farther I bend over, the more the ribbon is going to ride up high on my ass and bare myself to him.

But even as I experience the thrill of excitement over the position he's putting me in, a wave of anxiety hits me hard. My chest tightens and my muscles tense all over. My hands are practically shaking between nerves, fear, and desire as those emotions battle within me.

I consider pushing back against him, refusing to give him my backside. I know it will immediately ease my fear because I do not fuck doggy style.

Never.

Not since that night.

I'm betting the few partners I've had just assumed that means I'm just too vanilla for that, or maybe they just don't care as long as they get to fuck me, but I've never been pressured before to do it. Only one guy had an issue with it, and he ultimately declared me too boring in bed to satisfy his needs when I refused.

Of course, he only said that after he fucked me missionary and got his rocks off.

But as much as this situation concerns me, there's an equal part that is curious. My fight-or-flight response would normally gear me to flight, too terrified to do anything that would too closely resemble those vague flashes of memory that haunt me.

But Beck has proven to be different. That was apparent the minute he made me orgasm that first time, and thus there is a part of me that has formed a measure of trust in him to not hurt me. This part of Sela Halstead wants to push at my boundaries even though I'm scared shitless to do so.

With a deep breath, I take a moment to also remind myself that I don't want to do anything to turn Beck off. I don't want him to lose interest in me, and thus lose my tenuous connection he gives me to Townsend. So as if that sentiment almost gives me permission to explore my desire for him, I decide to let Beck have his way with me from a position where I can't see a damn thing he's doing to me.

My hands lower to the dark Danish teak wood to support myself and I lower my torso until my ribbon-covered breasts are mashed against the table. I turn my head to the side, rest my cheek against the cool surface, and stare out the window at the twinkling lights of the Bay Bridge. I take deep breaths to try to calm my racing heart, which is fueled in equal parts by apprehension and desire.

"I think this might be the most beautiful and amazing gift I've ever been given," he says, and I know he's knelt behind me as I can feel his warm breath from those words whisper against the flesh between my legs.

He doesn't touch me though, and doesn't say another word, which makes my heart pound harder. I only feel the warmth of his breath fluttering and I start to tense with anticipation.

Crack.

His palm comes down on my right ass cheek with the force of what feels like a sonic boom. It scares me so badly I scream, "Fuck!" and push upward from the table, but then just as quickly groan and flop back down when he sinks a finger inside of me.

My legs start to buckle as Beck runs his lips over the stinging skin on my butt and his finger moves gently in and out of my pussy. He bares his teeth, bites my flesh, and murmurs against me, "That was for the old man comment."

I laugh for just a brief moment, almost hysterically, as I realize with relief that he just spanked me and it wasn't all that bad. But then it's not so funny anymore when his finger is gone and his tongue takes its place. He works at me from behind, finally bringing his hands into play to help spread my legs farther with extreme gentleness.

Beck groans in delight as he licks and sucks at me, making it sound as if I'm the most delicious present he's ever had. No matter how many times he has had his mouth on me down there, I still always marvel at his voracious appetite and his clear love of making me come this way. The man has some serious oral skills.

"Christ, Sela," Beck says as he pulls his mouth away from me and replaces his tongue with two fingers now. "You're so wet. You're pussy is fucking begging for my cock, isn't it?"

I nod against the wood, but just so he knows my thoughts are still with him, I whisper, "*I'm* begging for it, Beck."

He laughs darkly, pushes his fingers in extra deep, but just as quickly they're gone as I feel him stand up behind me.

An undercurrent of panic fills me when I hear him tearing open a condom packet and the sound of his belt being pulled free of his pants. When his hands grab on to my hips, I have to suppress the urge to scramble away from him. The only other time a man has been behind me, he fucked me in the ass with no lube, and it tore me up so bad I bled terribly. I imagine it was quite the surprise to the doctors who worked on me in the hospital when I was brought in bleeding from my wrist, to find blood in my panties as well.

The looks of pity on their faces . . .

My eyes prick with unwanted tears and I blink against them furiously. I want to tell him to stop, or maybe to just be careful with me, but then the tip of his cock is being pressed to my pussy. Immediate relief and lust slam into me so powerfully that I actually have to suppress the urge to ram myself backward onto his shaft. This is proof positive that Beck North has definitely broken through some barriers I have with regard to sex.

"Happy birthday," I tell him again softly, a tacit permission for him to do with his present what he wants, but also to myself. It's permission to myself that I'm allowed to enjoy this.

He doesn't disappoint, punching his hips forward and filling me up in one seamless stroke.

I cry out from the force of the pleasure that rockets through my body.

"Fuck yeah," Beck groans, and immediately sets a quick pace. The feel of his length moving in and out of me, the friction and sounds, the smell of his cologne and the extinguished candles in the air. It all makes me dizzy with lust, hungry to get him to completion, and an almost savage need he's created within me for a nuclear orgasm that apparently only he can hand out to me.

Beck pounds inside of me, the head of his cock hitting that most sensitive spot, and my orgasm curls inward before blowing apart. I cry out his name, as it's become my habit to do so, and it causes Beck to plant deep as he starts to come right along with me, and all I can think is that this is the best feeling in the entire world.

He bends his body, curls around me, his hands slipping around my waist. His labored breath ruffles at my hair and I can't help but smile when he murmurs, "Best. Birthday. Ever."

CHAPTER 12

Beck

I cut two slices of the cake that Sela bought, and even though I detest raspberry, I know I'll give my best groan of pleasure when it hits my tongue so she knows how much I appreciate what she's done. I cannot even remember the last time someone recognized my birthday, outside of Linda giving me a card each year and Caroline calling me on my birthday, which is way better than a card.

My parents, the cold, emotionless robots that they are, never celebrated birthdays in an intimate way. When Caroline and I were younger, they would, of course, throw huge parties and invite everyone in their social circle. There would be ostentatious food, pony rides, clowns, bouncy houses, and a gazillion presents for Caroline and me. But that wasn't really for us. That was for show.

It was a way for our parents to prove to the world that they were good and benevolent, and that my younger sister and I were well cared for. As we got a bit older, the parties stopped but the expensive gifts didn't. I was given a Porsche for my sixteenth birthday. Caroline received a Mercedes convertible. When we both reached adulthood, we got access to our trust funds and only the impersonal birthday card sent from my mother's or father's secretary.

As per usual this year, I got a card from Linda and a card two days late from my parents. Caroline called me on my birthday while I was at work, and she then put Ally on the phone, who sang "Happy Birthday" to me. Until today, that had been my favorite birthday memory.

But as much as I love my niece, and she was beyond adorable singing to me on the phone, I'm sorry . . . Sela's gift was infinitely better.

Not just because it was sex, because, hello . . . sex. Sex is amazing in and of itself. Sex with Sela is beyond compare. Taking her bent over my dining room table, listening to her little moans and feeling her push back against me so I'd give it to her deeper? That was absolutely mind-blowing.

But that's not why it's my favorite.

It's my favorite because while I've only known Sela for a week, I've learned enough to know that what she did tonight was way out of her comfort zone.

Sela, the frugal student, who is happier to have a tea kettle from me than a two-thousand-dollar Louis Vuitton purse. Sela, the confident woman, who is sexier in a pair of jeans and a T-shirt than in Victoria's Secret lingerie. Sela, the passionate introvert, who has yet to try to trap me with sexually overt moves and promises.

When I walked in tonight, saw her standing there in that ribbon, I did more than start to get hard for her. I felt a shift in my skepticism about the nature of women and the lengths they'll go to get what they want. I've seen firsthand how some women can take without ever giving a single thing in return, and still think they deserve more. But Sela stood before me, hesitantly offering me her body, not to get anything in return, but merely because she felt bad I had not celebrated my birthday.

Sela, the inexperienced, put herself out there with all the risk on her shoulders and the only motive to her plan that I have something just for myself.

It simply touched me.

"You didn't have to clean up," I hear from behind me, and turn to find Sela standing there in her normal sleep attire, her hair pulled on top of her head in a messy bunch and damp around her neck from the shower she just had. A simple black tank top and black cotton panties, skin dewy-looking from some peach-smelling lotion she slathers on, and it's the sexiest thing I've ever seen. Of course, she comes to bed each night wearing something similar, and each night she ends up naked by my hands.

I wonder if there will ever come a day where she just gives in to the naked part and ditches the cute but sexy sleepwear. Will it happen this week, since my birthday surprise shows she's coming out of her shell a bit? Or maybe it will take a few more weeks to get truly comfortable? A few months?

I stop my brain in midthought and just blink at Sela in confusion. Am I actually considering more than our planned month together?

The immediate thought *doesn't* strike fear in my heart.

Interesting.

"I cut us each a slice of cake," I tell her as I grab a fork from the drawer and hand it to her, followed by a plate filled with chocolate and raspberry—gag—goodness. "And I didn't mind cleaning up the kitchen. You went to a lot of effort on my behalf."

"Yeah, but it's your birthday celebration, so you shouldn't have to do anything tonight," she points out as she dips the fork into the cake. She puts it in her mouth, closes her eyes, and moans. "I love chocolate and raspberry together."

And fuck . . . that little moan. So goddamn sexy it makes me want knock the plate out of her hand and drag her to the floor.

Instead, I clear my throat and pick up the slice I had cut for myself, intent on eating the cake without gagging. "So what do you want to do the rest of the evening?"

Sela raises her eyebrows in surprise, because that is an unusual question. Our normal evenings are I come home, we go out to eat or eat in, and then we fuck for hours until we fall asleep.

"Whatever you want to do," she says while sinking her fork back into the cake. "It's your birthday party."

I break off a tiny piece of the cake with the least raspberry on it and scoop it up. "Well, normally I'd say let's get naked and get in bed, but we do that pretty much every night. How about we just hang out?"

I can tell this completely stuns Sela, because her face clouds with skepticism. I smile at her and put the fork into my mouth, pull in the offensive-tasting crap, and chew. Sela watches me and her eyes narrow, getting ready to call bullshit on me for just wanting to hang out and not just get to the hot and dirty fucking.

"You hate the cake, don't you?" she accuses, sex completely forgotten.

I stare at her midchew and force a swallow. "What? No, of course not."

"You totally hate it," she says while pointing a finger at me. "I can tell by the look on your face."

"You're imagining things."

"Oh yeah," she fires back with a mischievous grin. "Then eat some more. Right now. In fact, eat the whole thing."

God, she's fucking cute.

I grin back at her and turn to set the plate down on the counter. "Okay, I hate raspberry. You got me."

She winces and lifts her shoulders in apology. "Sorry. I wasn't sure what you'd like and I just thought everyone on this planet liked chocolate and raspberry together. Are you sure you're not an alien?"

"I like chocolate just fine. Vanilla or even strawberry. But raspberry, no." I shudder just to prove my point.

"You're so weird," she says, and takes another bite.

"So, want to just hang out tonight?" I ask her, enjoying this little interchange.

"No sex?" she asks to clarify.

"Of course there's going to be sex," I scoff at her. "But not until later. We can watch TV, listen to music, play cards, go out for a drink. Whatever you want."

Sela takes one more bite of cake, chews, then swallows. She hands me the plate and says, "You take that, and I'm going to go brush my teeth so you don't have to taste raspberry on me."

"What makes you think I'll be tasting raspberry on you?" I tease as she walks away. "I just want to talk and hang out. I don't plan on kissing you or anything."

She doesn't even look at me as she saunters down the hall, her ass swaying and those black panties exposing the bottom cheeks that's fucking sexy as hell. "Oh, you're going to kiss me all right. You're not going to be able to help yourself."

I laugh to myself as I turn to scrape the remainder of her cake into the garbage, because fuck if she isn't right about that.

"Okay, are you ready?" I ask Sela as I reach into the box. I pull a card out and wait for her to choose.

She sits on the opposite end of the couch from me, still wearing her black tank top and panties, which are obviously distracting. Her back is pressed up against the armrest and her long legs are stretched out, one ankle crossed over the other. They press up against my jean-clad legs as I sit at the opposite end of the couch, with my back flush against the armrest as well.

Sela nibbles on her fingernail and says, "Sports and Leisure."

We were too lazy to play a full game of Trivial Pursuit, so we're just taking turns reading trivia questions to each other. If we get the answer wrong, we owe sexual favors to the other. Or at least that was the original premise when we started, but both of us kind of suck at this, the favors mounting up. But it's really moot anyway, since we never seem to have a problem bestowing favors on each other.

My eyes scan down the card to the orange circle with "SL" in the middle and I read out loud to her, "What do Las Vegas blackjack dealers stand on?"

Her eyebrows furrow and she nibbles harder on her nail. With a shrug of her shoulders she says with a great deal of uncertainty, "A stool?"

I bust a gut laughing the minute those words come out of her beautiful mouth. The card falls to my lap and my hands go to my stomach because I'm laughing so hard it hurts. Sela gives me an exasperated look, leans forward, grabs the card from where it rests on my right thigh, and reads the answer out loud. "Seventeen?"

I snap my mouth shut, choke down a snicker, and stare at her.

"I don't get it," she says in a confused voice, and I almost fall off the couch laughing again. She uncrosses her legs, raises her knees, and kicks out at me with a mock snarl of outrage. "What's so funny?"

Straightening up, I get myself under control and tell her, "Seventeen is the number at which a blackjack dealer must stop taking hits."

"I still don't get it," she says more forcefully. "And I think the way the question was worded that 'stool' was a logical answer."

A snort pops out, and I tamp it down so I don't lose it again. "Have you ever played blackjack before?"

She shakes her head.

"Poker? Spades? Rummy?" I ask, throwing out popular card games.

She shakes her head again but adds on with a mischievous grin, "I've played Monopoly before. I'm actually quite good at that."

Chuckling, I grab her by the ankles and pull her legs back down so she relaxes. I smooth my palm up and down her calf, actually petting her in a casual way that denotes we're still relaxing. If it was something more than relaxing, my hand would be moving higher up in between her thighs, but I'm content for now.

Very content, actually.

"Have you ever been to Vegas?" I ask her, my hand now moving to her foot. I glance down at her toes, coated in a light purple color. I pick her foot up and start to massage it.

She groans and her head tilts back when she says, "Never been. Any fun?"

"For some people," I tell her. "If you like gambling, cheesy shows, and all-you-can-eat buffets, none of which I really like."

"I think it's a given I wouldn't be much of a gambler," she says as she brings her eyes to me.

"We should go," I say suddenly. "This weekend. I'll show you all you need to know and then you can say you've experienced Vegas."

Sela does nothing but stare at me a moment with a blank face. Then she very carefully, very neutrally says, "This is getting a little off track, don't you think?"

My hand goes still against her arch. "What do you mean?"

She pulls her foot away and raises both knees again, sitting up straighter on the couch. She wraps her arms around her shins and stares at me with worry in her blue eyes. "It's just . . . as your Sugar Baby, I'm sort of here to serve you. We both know that means sex, but it also means if you want me to go somewhere with you as your date, I'll do that too."

"Okay," I say, because that's pretty accurate, although I hate the fucking title of Sugar Baby, and I sure as shit don't want to be thought of as a Sugar Daddy. I don't need to fucking pay for a woman to want to be with me. "So what's the problem?"

"You don't want to go to Vegas. You want *me* to go and experience it because I haven't yet."

"Pretty much," I agree with her, still befuddled as to what point she might be trying to make.

Sela drops her chin to the top of one knee and I swear I see guilt-filled eyes staring back at me. "You don't have to do nice things for me, Beck. You already gave me all I could ever hope for when you paid for my education. I don't need anything else."

An intense sensation of sadness fills me now that Sela has made her point. And I'm sad because she's exactly right. I don't owe her anything more than what I've given. I certainly shouldn't be concerned with whether or not she's been to Vegas.

But fuck it.

I can't help myself.

"You gave me a birthday celebration," I throw out to her. "That is totally outside of a normal Sugar Baby's duties."

Sela rolls her eyes. "That was sex."

"No," I say firmly as I lean forward, grab her wrists, and pull on her. She comes up to her knees and falls forward onto me when I keep pulling. "You did that because you were horrified my parents sent a generic, stamped card two days late."

"Well, that's not really—"

"And you wanted to do something nice for me. You went shopping, cooked dinner, got me a cake and a present, and the present, I have to say, was really, really good. Probably my favorite ever."

"But I fucked up on the raspberry," she points out with a smile as she lies on top of me, her hands resting on either side of my chest.

"The point I'm trying to make is that you and I do not have a conventional 'sugarship'—I've got to get someone in marketing to change that name. It's stupid as fuck."

"Agreed," she says.

"About 'sugarship' being stupid as fuck?"

"Well, yes I do agree with that, but more so about this not being very conventional."

"So to bring this full circle," I say as I put my hands under her armpits and drag her up my body a little higher. "I say we sort of make this whatever we want. If you want to do something nice for me, that's awesome. If I want to take you to Vegas to show you the sights, that's awesome too. Let's sort of make this our own thing."

Sela's eyes get soft and I realize I've never seen her look so tender before. There's always a part of this woman that I feel is held in reserve. She nods in agreement with me, but then brings me slightly back to reality when she says, "At least for the next few weeks until our agreement is up."

I'm not sure how I really feel about that, but it's not something to debate tonight, so I merely nod. "Until our agreement is up."

CHAPTER 13

Sela

Even though I've been in the corporate headquarters of Townsend-North Holdings once before, I'm still a bit intimidated by the grandeur of the lobby. Townsend-North is the parent company that owns The Sugar Bowl. I'm not sure what else it owns, as I've never talked "business" with Beck, but whatever their empire encompasses, it makes so much money that it practically oozes up out of the marble flooring.

The other time I'd been here was to meet my "friend" Karla Gould for lunch. That was the day I'd gotten a peek inside JT's office and imagined me driving a letter opener into his brain. Had he actually been sitting in there, I wonder if I would have been compelled to attack because that fantasy was so vivid. Just thinking about it now sends a shiver of excitement up my spine. Not the type of shiver I get from Beck. Not even close, actually, but it's still a pleasant, tingly feeling that most certainly doesn't turn me off.

I walk up to the receptionist station, which looks to be hand-carved from a light-colored wood that's polished to a high sheen with muted brushed silver accenting. The black granite top with silver flecks matches the black marble flooring that my tennis shoes squeak against. As I look down to the noisy suckers, I think for a split second that perhaps I should have dressed up to come see Beck at his office.

But then I immediately discount it. I don't need to impress him at this point, and besides . . . when he texted me about an hour ago inviting me to lunch, I was just finishing up one of my exams before fall break and didn't have time to run back to the condo to get changed. He'll have to accept me as is, although I did take a bit of time this morning to put a little makeup on. I find myself doing that more and more often, and only because I shamefully want to look pretty for Beck.

Shameful indeed.

Calling attention to myself like that.

Today is my sixteenth birthday.

I was raped.

I think I deserved it.

A shudder runs through me as I think about that entry in my journal, and I burn from the inside out with mortification. While I don't remember much about what happened to me at that party—just memory flashes and, of course, medical records documenting my injuries—I do remember much of what led up to that party. The humiliation today is as strong as it was ten years ago when I realized that I brought it all down upon myself by trying to play big girl in a harsh man's world.

I swallow hard, give myself a mental shake to get it together, and smile at the receptionist, who is stunningly beautiful with vivid red hair arranged in an elegant chignon and peridot green eyes that glow almost eerily. Those have to be contacts.

"Can I help you?" she asks crisply.

"I'm here to see Beck North."

Clarista—I see her by her nameplate—slides her gaze down

my body, taking in my casual attire and actually wrinkles her nose at me. "Let me just verify that with his secretary before I send you back. Your name?"

"Sela Halstead," I tell her, trying to muster confidence within myself. I straighten my spine and even throw my shoulders back so she can perhaps see my fantastic tits—according to Beck—and that they are natural, unlike hers.

She actually turns her back on me, speaking in a low voice into the phone as she calls who I assume to be Beck's secretary. I know her name is Linda because he told me last night that she's the only person other than his sister who actually recognizes his birthday. He said she's like his surrogate grandmother or something, and I find that fascinating that she works for a man who essentially peddles flesh—in a legal manner, of course.

Clarista turns back to me and flashes a tight smile as she stands from behind the desk. "Follow me."

I walk behind her to a closed door with a security panel attached to the wall beside it. She pulls at a security fob attached to her waist that stays connected by a retractable chain, and holds it up to the panel. A small red light blinks once and then turns green. She opens the door, looks down her nose at me, and says, "You can head straight down this hall. Linda will meet you."

"I know my way," I say, and turn from her, now actually feeling a little bit of excitement about seeing Beck. I find it strange and fascinating over the ways in which he's seemingly commandeered my attention. I've never been excited to see a man before. I most definitely have never enjoyed sex like this before.

And damn . . . last night . . . just sitting on the couch and laughing while we read trivia questions to each other; it was almost surreal. It was the closest I've ever truly come to maybe having a normal relationship with a man where conversation flowed freely and without effort.

Putting aside the fact that he's paid me a great deal of money to sit on that couch with him, of course.

A woman of about sixty I'd guess steps into the main hall from an intersecting one, and I have to assume it's Linda. She's a little on the heavy side but is wearing a stylish pantsuit of navy blue with a blue, red, and gold checked scarf tied at her neck. Her hair is snowy white and her eyes a soft brown. She gives me a warm smile as I approach and holds her hand out. "You must be Sela. Beck told me you were going to steal him away for lunch today."

I'm immediately taken in by her warm affection for her boss, and as I shake her hand, I tell her, "It's nice to meet you."

She squeezes my hand and then she lets her gaze slide down my body and back up again, except there's not a hint of condescension or judgment. She smiles at me brilliantly and says, "Aren't you just the loveliest of creatures. Beck really lucked out with you."

My face flames red because I don't know that I've ever been paid a more genuine compliment in my life, and I'm more than a little shamefaced that if she knew my ulterior motive, she'd never think Beck lucked out with me.

I follow Linda back down a hall, we turn down another, and I recognize the area. She leads me to a corner office, and as I peer down the corridor that runs the length of the building, I can see the corner of Karla's desk from where I stand. JT's office is right beside that.

Linda opens the door and motions me in. "Beck is actually downstairs meeting with the programmers. He's running a few minutes late but he'll be here soon. Just make yourself comfortable."

"Thank you," I murmur as I step in, taking in Beck's office. It's as pristine, contemporary, and minimalist as his home is. There are no personal photos or knickknacks. The decor is in black, white, and gray with some modern artwork on the walls that look like nothing more than splashes of paint in yellows, oranges, and reds.

I wonder if the impersonal nature of his home and work space have anything to do with what seems to be the sterile familial environment he grew up in. I know my family didn't have a lot in the way of money, but we certainly had love within our tiny house. While I was closest to my mother, who was very young when she had me, I also have an affectionate bond with my dad, which briefly got stronger right after my mom died three years ago, but then began to cool a little when he started dating again. He's now been with Maria for a year and I expect they'll get married soon. I don't begrudge him that, and Maria's nice enough, but after Mom died, Dad was all I had left and now I have to share him. That I don't like very much.

"Well, what do we have here?" I hear from behind me, and my skin immediately turns icy with apprehension and loathing.

I turn around to see Jonathon Townsend standing in the doorway to Beck's office. His hands are tucked casually into the pockets of very expensive navy tailored slacks and his eyes drop to my breasts, which fill out my vintage Pepsi long-sleeved T-shirt quite well.

He clearly doesn't even remember me from when I introduced myself to him almost two weeks ago. The way he's eyeing me creeps me the hell out, and when he takes a step into the office, I have to resist the urge to bolt behind Beck's desk.

Get it together, Sela. You can't be afraid of this man. You intend to kill him, after all, so you have to be comfortable in his presence.

"I'm Sela Halstead," I say, proud to find my voice sounds strong and not shaky like my insides feel. "We met at the mixer weekend before last."

He carelessly shrugs his shoulders, indicating he doesn't remember, nor does he care that he doesn't remember. This fills me with a low, bubbling fury, because this man raped me and yet he stands no more than five feet from me without a hint of recognition. My fingers curl into fists and the urge to attack and claw his eyes out almost causes my legs to give way.

Townsend takes two more steps toward me, almost in a slithering fashion, and raises his eyes from my boobs to my face. He gives me what I know he thinks is a charming grin, and says, "I can't believe I don't remember. I'm almost disappointed in myself."

I hold my eyes straight on him, resisting the urge to roll them, and without a care in the world if this hurts my plans at some point. "Well, luckily I met Beck shortly thereafter, so it all worked out perfectly."

You scummy, motherfucking, amoral, sick evil bastard.

Having such a huge ego and not realizing that was an insult to him, he reaches a hand out to touch me. Not sure if he's aiming for my face, my hair, or maybe a breast squeeze, but I take a hasty step back.

"Skittish little thing," he murmurs, and I can see that turns him on by the sizzle in his eyes.

Bile rises in my throat even as I go into fight mode. I prepare myself to launch a foot to his nuts if he reaches again and I even think, *I wonder if there's a letter opener on Beck's desk I can use to finish the job*, but then Beck's voice floats over me like a protective blanket. "Sela? Everything okay?"

I tilt my head to the right, look past JT, and see Beck striding in looking none too happy to see his partner standing there. I scurry around Townsend and my relief is evident by the now-clear shaking in my voice, "Hey . . . ready to go to lunch?"

He narrows his eyes at me as he just clearly heard in my tone everything I was hoping to hide. Fear, anxiety, relief.

His gaze snaps to JT, pinning him with hard eyes. While he's focused on his partner, his question is to me. "What's going on here?"

The tension is thick and I have no clue what to say. I certainly don't want to cause trouble, but JT just suavely chuckles and walks past both of us. "Just introducing myself."

Beck and I turn our bodies slightly to watch him walk to the door. JT stops just before exiting and turns to me. His gaze is lewd, directed only to me, and in a low voice he says, "It was a pleasure to meet you, Sela. I hope to see *more* of you."

My entire body shudders and I can see Beck visibly tighten next to me. Without a lick of respect to Beck's business partner and with no care in the world if this offends Beck, I tell JT, "I wish I could say the same."

Beck's head snaps toward me, but I don't take my eyes of JT. I can't afford to ever give him my lowered gaze or my fear, as devious as he's proven to be, and I want him to know I am not intimidated by him.

JT just laughs and turns to walk out the door, pulling it shut behind him. The minute he's gone from my sight, I let out a sigh of relief and feel my shoulders relax.

Beck threads his fingers through my hair, curling his hand around the back of my head. With worried eyes, he bends toward me and asks in a menacing voice, "Did he do something to you?"

I shake my head. "No, it's just . . . he was coming on to me and it was pretty creepy."

"Asshole," Beck snarls.

I give a nervous laugh. "I have to say . . . I don't like your partner very much."

"Makes two us," he says, and I blink in surprise. Beck and I haven't discussed JT before other than that first night we met when he told me that JT didn't like confident women, and so I've never known what his feelings were. For all I knew, they were the tightest and best of friends.

Stepping in to Beck, I press my forehead briefly to his chest and say, "Well, I'm glad you came in when you did. I was getting ready to kick him in the balls."

"I would have paid money to see that," he says with a laugh, and then with a tug against my hair pulls my head from him. He tilts my face back and gives me a light kiss filled with nothing but affection.

It's nice.

Very nice.

"Hungry?" he asks with a smile.

"Starved."

"Good, let's go."

Beck takes me by the hand, laces our fingers together.

This is also very nice and I actually get a warm feeling within my chest as we walk out of his office, and Linda's eyes immediately take notice of us holding hands. She gets almost misty-eyed as she smiles at us.

"Get that look off your face, woman," Beck growls, but it's done with a great deal of fondness.

Linda puts her hand over her mouth, looks at Beck with shining eyes, and shakes her head slightly at what she clearly thinks is a miracle going on in front of her. "I can't help it. You two are adorable."

"Christ," Beck mutters, and pulls me past her desk.

I chuckle and give a tiny wave to Linda over my shoulder.

When we hit the lobby, Beck drops my hand but immediately drapes his arm around my shoulder, pulling me into him and laying a kiss to my temple before murmuring, "You're going to be setting all the gossips' tongues wagging with your visit here today."

My eyes cut over to the coldly beautiful Clarista, who watches Beck and me with her mouth hanging open. I can't help it: I put my arm around his waist and step in closer to him as we walk by her desk, and shoot her a sweet smile. "Goodbye, Clarista. It was lovely to meet you."

Beck looks over to Clarista, squeezes me in closer. Clarista's eyes move to Beck, almost pleading with him to tell her this isn't happening. Beck North, the most eligible bachelor in this building, is cavorting with a girl in a T-shirt and Converse shoes.

"I was just going to step out for a bite of lunch, but now that I think about it, I'm going to take the rest of the day off," Beck says impetuously to Clarista. "Will you let Linda know?"

"Yes, Mr. North," she says, her voice completely dumbfounded.

"Excellent," Beck says with a grin, and then he pulls me closer as we walk out of the lobby.

CHAPTER 14

Beck

"Is this weird?" Sela asks as she smooths down the dress at her hips with nervous hands.

"No, and quit fidgeting," I tell her as I guide her into the ballroom by the elbow.

"It seems weird," she maintains.

"It's not weird," I tell her for about the hundredth time. "And we don't have to stay long. Just enough to make an appearance and then we can go."

"See, I told you it was a waste of money to buy this dress," she complains as we walk toward the bar. "Silly, since you only have to stay for a little while. I should have just stayed at the condo and waited for you, and you could have saved yourself a pretty penny."

I laugh and squeeze her elbow. "Ever-practical Sela."

God, her practicality is fucking adorable. When I told Sela at lunch a few days ago that The Sugar Bowl had another mixer that I needed to attend, she first got jealous on me. Oh, it was barely perceptible . . . a tightening of her jaw, a spark in her eye. I wanted to call her out on it but knew it would embarrass her, so I quickly let her know that I wanted her to go with me as my date. I assured her that I just had to make an appearance and that we wouldn't stay long.

So after lunch that day, we then went shopping for a cocktail dress. I let Sela pick out what she wanted, and while the boutique I took her to didn't have anything that cost less than a thousand dollars, I was surprised she picked a more sedate dress. It's champagne-colored silk with sleeves that sit off her shoulders, a snug-fitting bodice, and a skirt that falls below her knees. It's actually quite elegant and not at all something a Sugar Baby would wear, which means I loved the fuck out of it.

Tonight she paired it with a pair of high heels in the same champagne color and put her hair in a tight twist at the back of her neck. She looks like she could be attending a fancy charity dinner instead, and I realize as we walk into the ballroom that my chest is actually puffed out a little with pride in the woman that is with me.

We step up to the bar and a bartender swoops in on us taking our drink orders. I offer an empty stool to Sela. How she so gracefully gets on it with that tight skirt is beyond me, but when she crosses one leg over the other and a long slit appears running up her thigh, I immediately understand. I can't help myself . . . placing my fingers on her bare skin and running them up high until the material comes together again.

"You are the sexiest woman in this room," I tell her as I tilt my head to the side and kiss her bare shoulder. She shivers and lets out a tiny gasp of pleasure.

I pull back and grin at her, finding her looking at me with confusion.

"How do you do that?" she asks in amazement.

"Do what?"

"Make me feel like some high school girl with a crush on the cutest boy in the class and he just looked at her and made her go all silly inside," she replies.

"I know the feeling," I tell her softly, and she smiles at me.

A rare, genuine, full smile from Sela with nothing else hidden underneath. It captivates me and everything else in the room melts away. Our eyes lock and hold. I feel an almost electric current pop between us, as if I've just had an epiphany of some sort.

But then Sela's gaze wavers and slides past my left shoulder, narrows for an instant, and then fills with disgust. I turn my body that way, look over my shoulder, and immediately see what caused that look.

The bar is curved like a horseshoe and JT is standing at the end about six stools down from Sela and me. He's got his arm around the back of one of the stools that holds a scantily clad and huge-chested blond girl, early twenties as best I can tell, and he's whispering into her ear. She's clearly his target for tonight.

JT takes his hand, drops it to her waist, and then slides it up her ribs. She giggles, shifts in her seat and moves her arm giving him more access. He slides it higher and his fingers brush the outside of her breast. She now turns coy, bats his hand away, and laughs again. JT doesn't laugh though and puts his hand right back at her ribs.

It's a classic show of dominance, and I've seen it so many times before.

"He's really got the moves, doesn't he?" Sela murmurs beside me.

I don't turn to look at her but continue to watch JT in almost mesmerized disgust. "I take it that's your sarcastic voice, right?"

She laughs. "That obvious, huh?"

JT goes for another touch to the woman's breast and she again pushes his hand away, but laughs flirtatiously as she does it. I want to tell her she's doing nothing more than pissing him off, but what good would it do? Any Sugar Baby in this room with the exception of Sela isn't going to pass up a chance with JT.

Our bartender returns with our drinks, dirty martini for Sela and scotch for me. I hold my glass out to hers and we tap the edges together. "Cheers."

"Cheers."

Sela pulls the toothpick out loaded with three olives and pulls one off with her teeth. It's a sexy move and I'm fascinated by it until she points the toothpick now holding two olives at JT. "You know . . . I have to wonder, do you see any good in your partner at all?"

It's not a strange question, but her tone has an odd inflection. Almost combative in nature. I know Sela doesn't like JT, and shit . . . I don't like him much nowadays, but it seems a bit personal to Sela. I look over at him, start to turn back to Sela to tell her the truth of my feelings when I watch the blonde push up off the stool and grab her purse. She goes on tiptoe, whispers something in JT's ear, and then heads off toward the bathroom. JT watches her for a moment, his eyes pinned to her ass, and then he turns back to the bar. Reaching inside his left breast pocket, he pulls something out.

He does it so swiftly and assuredly I almost don't believe what I'm seeing. He casually holds his hand over the woman's drink and a white powder floats down into it. He looks quickly at the bartender, whose back is turned, and then picks up the drink to swirl the powder until it's dissolved.

"Did he just—" Sela starts to ask, but I'm already pushing away from the bar like an enraged bull.

I stalk toward JT in angry strides, watching as he stares at the drink that he's now set onto the bar with a satisfied smile. Just when I'm a foot away from him, his head comes up and makes eye contact with me. He smiles at first in welcome, but when he sees the look on my face, it slides right back off.

I grab the drink, step up on the foot rail at the bottom of the bar, and lean over it, pouring the drink out into the sink on the other side.

"What the fuck?" JT says with indignation.

I slam the glass down and my hand shoots out, grabbing a fistful of JT's shirt and tie. I haul him away from the bar and start pulling him toward the exit. People scramble out of our way, most with looks of surprise that the two owners of The Sugar Bowl seem to be on the verge of a fistfight.

He tries to shrug me off but I hiss at him, "You follow me the fuck out of here right now, asshole, or so help me God I'm going to call the police over what you just tried to do."

JT immediately goes still and I give him a hard shove toward the exit as I release my hold on him. He goes stumbling for a moment, then catches his footing. He looks around at everyone staring and holds his hands up, "Nothing to worry about, folks. Just a friendly tug-of-war over a Sugar Baby."

He gives a smarmy grin, and the closest people who heard that laugh nervously. I don't laugh and give him a rough push to his shoulder, sending him stumbling again. That gets JT moving and we walk quickly out of the ballroom. JT doesn't look at me but walks directly to the men's bathroom. I follow him in and he turns to face me. I can tell by the quiet of the room that it's empty except for us and I lunge at him. Now grabbing fistfuls of shirt, jacket, and tie, I push him back across the tiled floor several steps until his back slams into the wall and he grunts from the pain.

"Jesus fucking Christ, Beck," he says, and I pull him away and slam him back again.

"You sick fuck," I snarl at him. "You just fucking tried to roofie that girl. What in the ever-loving fuck is wrong with you?"

I am so furious right now I almost feel like I could kill JT. I see the glaze in his eyes from drugs and alcohol, imagine what he would have done to that girl tonight, and I see my entire empire starting to crumble down around me. I see nothing of the man I thought I knew within his fogged gaze. A man that I thought was just like me, but I'm starting to realize was nothing more than a foolish pipe dream.

"Relax, bro," he says calmly. "It was just to loosen her up."

"You goddamn idiot motherfucker," I yell at him, and drop my hands away. I raise one up, point to him, and see it's shaking. "You are going to bring us down, JT, and I'm tired of this shit. I want you out of this company. I want you gone and you can go do whatever sick, perverted shit goes on in that head of yours away from me, but I'm not about to let you pull me down with you."

"You can't force—"

I cut him off by grabbing him again, pulling him away from the wall, and slamming him back into it. His eyes go wide with fear. "Just shut the fuck up. Now I want you to walk your ass out of this hotel and get in a cab and go home. If I see you go back in that ballroom, I'm calling the cops and it's over for both of us."

It's not an empty threat this time. I'm now prepared to do whatever I need to do, ideally to get JT out of The Sugar Bowl, but at the least do what it takes to protect that woman tonight.

"Fine," he rasps out, and my hands drop. "Fine, I'll go."

"You be at the office tomorrow at eight A.M. and be ready to iron this out," I tell him as I run my hands through my hair in frustration. "This shit is done, JT. I'm not kidding."

"Fine, okay . . . whatever," he says, holding up his hands in surrender. "I'll get it under control. I promise."

I point toward the door. "Go home, JT. Now."

He grabs onto his jacket at the lapel, pulls on the material to straighten it out. He then straightens his tie and nods. He turns toward the door and starts to walk out.

I remind him. "Tomorrow . . . eight A.M., JT. We're settling this."

"I'll be there," he mutters, and then he's gone.

I take a few moments, collect my thoughts, and take a few deep breaths, but I'm still shaking with anger and frustration as I head back into the ballroom. Sela sits at the bar, her eyes locked on me with worry the minute I walk back in.

When I reach her, her hand comes to my chest and she asks, "Is everything okay?"

I huff out a sigh, pick up my drink, and take a healthy slug. Setting the glass back down, I scrub my hand through my hair again and shrug. "I don't know."

Sela's hand grabs on to mine. She stands up from the stool and gracefully places her feet on the floor. Tugging at me, she says, "Come on . . . let's dance."

I don't want to fucking dance.

It's the last thing in the world I want at this moment, but I don't want to drop Sela's hand either, so I follow her in almost a trance out to the dance floor. When she reaches the middle and turns into my arms, I realize a song with a slow beat is playing. Sela steps into me and one of my arms goes automatically around her waist; the other takes her hand and brings it to my chest.

She curves one hand behind my neck and strokes me softly as she whispers in a reassuring voice, "Just relax and cool down."

I look down at her as she stares up at me with earnest eyes filled with concern. My heart rate immediately takes a nosedive as I feel her hand on my neck and smell her peach lotion. I let out a huge pent-up breath of frustration and then give her a tired smile. "Sorry you had to see that."

She shrugs and steps in closer to me. Her eyes are round, clear, and filled with respect. "Honestly . . . what you did. How quickly you reacted. It was the most amazing thing I think I've ever seen in my life."

I try to make light of it, because the way she's looking at me both embarrasses and humbles me. "I was just trying to impress you so you'd sleep with me tonight."

She gives a tinkling laugh, her eyes bright with amusement. "That was already a given, Mr. North."

I can't resist. I lean down, capture her lips with mine, and give her a slow kiss. She sighs into my mouth and my arm around her waist tugs her in tighter to me.

Feels so fucking good holding her like this.

Dancing.

Kissing.

Just magical.

I pull my lips from hers and before I can even comprehend what I'm doing, I tell her, "Let's do away with the agreement."

Sela jerks in surprise and her lips draw down in dismay. "You want to end things now?"

"God, no," I tell her quickly with a nervous laugh, reeling her back in close. "I mean . . . the time frame. It was only for a month. Let's do away with that."

"You want me to stay in your condo?" she asks hesitantly. "Like move in for real?"

"Well, yeah . . . sure," I say, now not completely positive what I want or if this is the right thing to do. "I mean . . . your stuff is there, why not?"

She rolls her eyes at me. "Well, gee, Mr. Romantic . . . how can a girl pass up that offer?"

I laugh, give her a quick kiss, and then tell her, "Sorry. That wasn't very suave. What I mean is that I don't want you to leave in two weeks when the agreement is over. Okay?"

Sela's blue eyes go a shade deeper as she stares at me in solemn consideration. Finally, she tips her head in agreement. "Okay. I can do that."

"Excellent," I say, and then bend down to kiss her again.

Sela rests her head against my shoulder and for a few moments we just sway back and forth to the music. Another thought strikes me. "Next week is Thanksgiving. My sister and niece are going to visit for a few days."

"Want me to go back to my apartment while they're here?" she asks quietly.

"What?" I ask startled as I push her away from me. Peering down at her I give her a chastising look. "I want you to meet them. I really want you to help me cook Thanksgiving dinner. I most certainly don't want you going back to your apartment."

She smiles at me again.

First in relief.

Then with happiness.

One of those unfiltered, genuine smiles where she gives me 100 percent of Sela Halstead.

And it's fucking brilliant.

CHAPTER 15

Sela

For the first time in just over six months, I actually consider letting go of my vengeance against JT.

For just a moment, I consider what would happen if I focused instead on what I have here with Beck. He's given me so much more than money for my education. He's given me pleasure and respect. He's given me self-worth. Beck has made it so that I don't consider myself a victim. Without the weight of victimization on my shoulders, I have to wonder why revenge would be needed. And what would happen if I let the anger and rage go and opened up the empty space left behind to Beck North. I think I understand, deep in my heart, that he'd fill that space up perfectly.

The thought is thrilling yet scary.

It's also short-lived, as I realize that Beck tonight saved a woman from JT's clutches. What about the next woman though? And the one after that?

Because while Beck may think this is an isolated incident with his partner, I happen to know that a zebra doesn't change its stripes.

When I saw JT boldly and assuredly sprinkle powder in that woman's drink, I was overcome with hopelessness for the situation, inundated with fear for the unsuspecting, and flooded with painful memories of shame and humiliation. My stomach curdled, nausea rose, and I watched in stunned fascination as Beck pushed away from the bar. It was almost as if he was in slow motion as he strode angrily up to JT and pulled him roughly away. I watched as he yelled and pushed his partner across the floor, his face livid and flushed red. Internally, I chanted to myself, *Kill him, kill him, kill him,* wanting Beck to be my avenging angel, and was disappointed I didn't see bloodshed before they walked out of my line of sight.

I considered following but was frozen to my seat. I shakily sipped at my martini until I finally just gulped it down before pushing the empty glass away. What if Beck right now called the police and JT was arrested? How would I ever get to him?

But maybe if that happened, I could come forward to the police with my story and he'd go down for my assault too. That wasn't ideal to me, because while I had briefly considered this route when I first realized who Jonathon Townsend was, I just as immediately discounted it because it didn't seem satisfactory enough for me. I needed to know the identity of all my rapists and there was no guarantee he'd give them up. I also don't want JT populating this earth. As much as the idea of him getting gang-raped in prison appeals to me, I want to snuff out his wretched life so his brand of evil no longer exists. Finally, I want to make JT suffer before I end him. I want him scared, and I want him just as terrified of me as I was of him. I want all of them to suffer, and while I can't bring down on them the same horrors they perpetrated on me, I can end their lives, and that was suffering, right? Not to get to live their evil, sociopathic lives?

After the martini flushed its warmth through me, I then briefly considered taking my purse and following them both out. Within that purse sat my Walther PPK.

Well, it was my mom's handgun, because given my psychiatric history, there's no way I'd ever be given a permit, but it's in my possession now. About a month after she died, my father and I went through all her stuff. We gave her clothing away to a homeless shelter and Dad insisted I get her modest collection of jewelry except for her wedding band. All of her knickknacks stayed in their exact places within my family home, except I've noticed over the past year that some of them have been packed away, and I think that might be Maria asserting her influence. I figure Dad has them boxed and ready for me when I want them.

There wasn't much left, but in addition to her jewelry, I got her gun. My parents have always had guns for as long as I can remember. I grew up shooting with them from the time I was a little girl, my dad often driving us up to Marin County on the weekends for target practice. Sometimes we'd hit McClure's Beach on early foggy mornings and shoot beer cans off driftwood. Other times we'd head into Mount Tamalpais State Park where it was easy to get away from people and shoot into the silent forest.

I was comfortable with the gun. Knew how to load and shoot it.

While my long-distance aim is probably shit because I haven't been able to target shoot given the illegality of my possession of this gun, I intend to be up close and personal with JT when I use it.

I won't miss.

But ultimately, before I could rashly stalk out of the ballroom and commit cold-blooded murder to ease my pain, Beck was walking back in toward me. His jaw was locked tight, his eyes dull and grim. With a swiftness that surprised me, thoughts of vengeance and bloody death just evaporated, and I was filled with an overwhelming concern for Beck and his peace of mind. There's no doubt he's troubled by what he saw, and there's also no doubt that when provoked, he's a man who will react quickly and harshly. My empathy for Beck actually overtook my hate of JT, and I was compelled to help ease his distress. Granted, dancing may have been a stupid idea, but it put us in an immediate situation where I could put my hands on him in a calming fashion.

Where he was tense and still vibrating with restrained anger when he took my hand in his and pressed the other into my lower back, within just moments of us touching each other, I felt his shoulders relax and his breathing even out. Right after that, Beck was inviting me to stay in his home on an indefinite basis and said we were scrapping the entire hoax of a sugarship that we had been perpetrating.

Then he invited me to cook Thanksgiving dinner with him.

To meet his sister and niece.

He was telling me that I was becoming important to him.

All things that I never imagined I'd gain when I started this quest.

And once again, I'm wondering if the path I'm on seeking retribution is a fool's errand when I consider what I can lose. Best-case scenario, I achieve my plans and get away with murder and Beck is never the wiser. We continue seeking a potential happily ever after.

Worst case, I get caught and spend my life in prison wondering if I lost something that may have had the potential to give me a normal and fulfilled life.

"You about ready to get out of here?" Beck asks gruffly, his hand rubbing sensuously on my lower back.

"If you are," I say as I pull my head off his shoulder and gaze up at him.

He smiles softly at me, tips his head down, and rubs his nose against mine. "I just really want to be alone with you. Away from all this shit."

With a slight tilt of my face, my mouth finds his and I answer with a tongue-filled kiss that causes him to groan and pull me in closer so I can feel the start of his erection burning through our clothes. The adrenaline, high emotions, and sexual longing in his eyes right now overwhelm me.

"Let's go," I murmur, and that's all he needs before he's leading me off the dance floor, through the ballroom, and out into the hotel lobby as he reaches into his pocket to pull out his cell phone. With a few quick taps, he dials his driver and merely says, "We're ready. Pull around."

Beck's hand is tight on mine as we step out into the chilly air. He doesn't say a word, but just stares intently down the street until he sees the limo rounding the block to pull up in front of us. He doesn't wait for the driver but pulls the back door open for me and helps me inside.

Crawling in right behind me, he tells the driver, "You can take us back to the Millennium, but circle the building when you get there until I tell you otherwise."

The driver barely gets, "Yes, sir," out before Beck is hitting the button that closes the window screen that separates us from him.

Beck lowers himself back on the seat beside me, and I gasp in surprise when he turns, puts hands to my hips, and drags me onto his lap so that my ass presses into his erection and my back into his chest. His arms circle my waist where he squeezes me briefly, places his lips to my ear, and whispers, "I need you right now. Can't wait."

My head spins and my entire body flushes hot with lust brought on not by the compromising situation he just put me in, but by the need in his voice. I answer by wiggling my butt and grinding down onto him.

Beck hisses, in pleasure . . . in pain . . . I don't know, but then his hands go to the hem of my dress and he roughly pulls the material up my legs, right past my hips where it bunches around my waist. No sooner is the dress out of his way than his hand is between my legs and his fingers are inching under the white cotton lace of my panties. No sooner is his hand in my panties than his fingers are against my clit, dipping inside me, massaging me in and out. My heels punch into the carpeted floor of the car, my legs straighten, and my back arches away from him as the back of my head presses into his shoulder for leverage.

"That's right," he growls as he finger-fucks me, moving his other hand over my chest to pinch at a nipple through the silk of my dress. "I want you to come on my hand, baby. Come for me, Sela."

My eyes roll into the back of my head as the pleasure threatens to consume me. His fiery touch, his filthy words, the mere fact he couldn't even wait until we pulled away from the hotel has me racing toward climax at Mach speed. I vaguely wonder if the driver knows what we're doing, figure he probably does, and God help me . . . that turns me on even more.

"Come on, Sela," Beck grits out, his stiff cock grinding into my ass from below. "Give it to me so I can fuck you. Please give it to me . . . I need inside you so bad."

And holy shit . . . I give it to him with a scream that reverberates through the limousine and no doubt that the driver heard that. My pelvis shoots up, grinds against his hand, and an animalistic groan of relief tears free.

"Oh, fuck me, that's hot," Beck says as he continues to rub circles around my clit while I shudder and shake in his embrace.

My head is still spinning, my body deliciously weak when Beck spins me in his arms, pulling me into a full straddle over his lap so I'm now facing him.

"Get my pants open," he huffs out urgently as his hand dives into his pocket for his wallet. I push up on my knees and quickly get his belt undone as he tries to get a condom out, both of our chests heaving with unrestrained fervor.

"Fuck," Beck barks out in frustration as he rifles through his wallet. "I don't have a goddamn condom."

My hands freeze and I raise my head to look at Beck. His face is awash with pain and need, and his voice cracks when he looks me right in the eye and says, "Christ . . . I want inside of you so fucking bad."

The sound I believe I hear is my stone heart cracking open even further in response to Beck. I hesitate only a moment before my hands start working again at his fly.

"Please, Sela," he croaks out as his fingers dig into my thighs. "Suck my dick . . . make this ache go away."

His zipper open, I pull at his pants, reach into his boxers, and take his cock from the material. It jumps in my hand and pearly pre-cum dribbles from the tip. I stare at him thick and hot and pulsing with need, squeeze him hard, and stroke up and down a few times.

Beck groans and his head falls back against the seat, eyes squeezed shut tight. "Please, Sela . . ."

"Shhh," I murmur low in my throat as I scramble backward off his lap. "I've got you."

His eyes open and he watches me with fascination as my knees hit the carpeted floor of the limo and I surge up over his lap. With one hand on his thigh, the other squeezing him around the root of his cock, I take the tip of him into my mouth and suck against him lightly. Beck moans in relief, and the fingers of both hands thread through my hair on either side of my head. He grips me lightly, his fingers pressing into my scalp as a means of holding me steady and not to force action.

This isn't the first time I've had Beck in my mouth, but it is the first time that I've truly wanted him there. The first time in my entire sexual life that I've seen the beauty of such an intimate act, and I take my time licking and sucking him so I can savor this experience. I'm torn between wanting to drive him wild and needing to end his suffering. As good as this feels to him in this exact moment, I want it to feel better to him in the next. So I squeeze, jack, lick, suck, hum, and flutter against his warm skin. I suck down the pre-cum he gives me and brace against his hands when the inevitable time will come that he'll pull me off his dick.

Beck is a considerate lover, and for whatever reasons, he's warned me every time before he's unloaded. He's never begrudged my unwillingness to swallow and has seemed satisfied with me stroking him to completion at the end.

I'm confident he'll give me the same courtesy here, but he'll be surprised to find it's not needed.

Not now.

Beck's hips start to punch upward, seeking more depth. He groans when I go down on him and grunts when I hollow my cheeks against the pull up. He calls my name when I slide my tongue down his shaft and curses loudly when I suck gently on his balls. As I stroke him faster at the base and bob my head with more vigor, Beck sounds like he's strangling.

Then comes the slight pull against my hair and he mutters, "Back off, Sela. Gonna come."

I grip him harder, take a deep breath, and plunge down so I

take him in deeply, move my other hand to stroke the skin behind his balls, and then suck hard on the way up.

"Holy fuck," Beck shouts as he orgasms and I nearly moan in satisfaction as I swallow everything he offers.

I swallow.

All of it.

And wish there was more, so I continue to suck against him.

"Oh, God, Sela," he groans as I keep squeezing and stroking, running my tongue around the fat head of his cock, trying to find any last droplets I might have missed.

His hands fall away from my head and find their way under my armpits, and then he's hauling me up. His dick falls away from my mouth and the next thing I know he's got me cradled on his lap with his face pressed into my neck. His breath is labored and I can feel his heart thundering under my hand as I lay it on his chest.

Beck's arms wrap around me and squeeze me tightly.

My own heart is racing right along with his and I'm high on the excitement of my new revelation.

An epiphany that will make me begin to question everything I thought I knew about myself.

I, Sela Halstead, am not as broken as I thought I was. While I thought Jonathon Townsend took everything away from me, I've realized just now that he took nothing. He only warped my perception.

Granted, I'm still pretty warped, but I learned something very important as Beck was coating my throat with his semen.

I realized that intimacy is actually something that I could learn to crave with a man like Beckett North and that I've only just begun to discover the true potential inside of myself.

CHAPTER 16

Beck

The alarm I set on my phone goes off faintly, as I made sure to turn the volume down before I went to sleep last night. I didn't want Sela to wake up, figuring she could use a solid, late sleep-in this morning.

After we got back from the Sugar Bowl Mixer last night, we ended up burning through three condoms throughout the night, because I fucking couldn't get enough of her. You would think with the almost seismic nature of the way I came down her throat that I would have been truly replete for the rest of the evening.

On the contrary, it's like the flame I had already burning on a steady low for Sela got whipped into a frenzied firestorm, and I couldn't leave her alone. I fucked her over and over again, my dick proclaiming clearly that it was in deep love with Sela's pussy. It was ready to move in, take up permanent residence, and never come out of hibernation again.

My hand reaches out, taps the screen on my phone to turn the alarm off, and I lay silently in the predawn gloom considering my situation at his very moment.

A naked, beautiful woman on top of me. Sela fell asleep a few hours ago, spread-eagled over my body right after she collapsed from the most recent fuck-fest. I swear . . . she came, I came, then she pitched forward onto my chest and was out like a light. Not sure what it says about the apparently whipped sap I'm becoming, but I wanted to leave her right there all night. Just let her lie on top of me, and I was ready to call it a day well completed and go to sleep myself.

But I didn't because my dick was deflating within her and I had a condom to dispose of. I gently eased out from under her, my cock actually feeling a little overused when it slipped free, and I quietly made my way into the bathroom to flush the rubber.

After a quick brushing of my teeth, I looked into the mirror and found that the man looking back at me didn't quite appear to be a confirmed bachelor anymore. No, tonight he had asked a woman to stay on in an indefinite basis in his house. Tonight, Beck North entered into his first true relationship with a woman, and if the quality of the orgasms that were had tonight are any indication of what's to come between us, I have to think it was a brilliant fucking decision on my part to invite Sela all the way in.

I padded back into the bedroom, turning the bathroom light off behind me. My first instinct was to slip into bed, roll Sela onto her side, and cuddle into her. I think they call it spooning.

Instead, I found myself inching toward her on my back, then I was pulling her back on top of me once I got settled. She let out a cute little moan, buried her face in my neck, and threaded her legs through mine. My arms came around her lower back and I held her tight against me. I had no problem falling asleep with her pinning me like that to the mattress.

This is a nice way to wake up, and if I had the time to do so, I'd slip my hand down over Sela's ass and play with her pussy for a bit until she woke up. But I don't have time, because I have to meet JT in an hour and a half and I want to get in before he does to get my thoughts in order.

Regretfully, I slip out from underneath Sela. She stirs, mutters a sleepy "Good Morning," and then rolls away from me. I smile, bend over, and kiss her on the back of the head before pulling the covers up over her.

Then I head into the bathroom to shower and get ready to take on my business partner in what will ultimately be a bitter grudge match between us.

I'm surprised when I get into the office at 7:30 A.M. that JT is already standing outside my office door and waiting for me. He holds a Styrofoam cup of coffee in one hand and a newspaper in the other. I'm also surprised to find him showered and fresh-looking without a hint of red in his eyes. I'm thinking extra squirts of Visine went into his appearance, and I know without a doubt this is carefully orchestrated by JT so that he isn't defending himself from a position of too much weakness.

He's showing me that he can present himself properly when warranted.

"Good morning," he says in an uncharacteristically humble voice, and it catches me off guard. I expected him to come out swinging with his first words.

"Morning," I say as I unlock my office door and turn on the lights. I walk directly to the minifridge hidden under the built-in liquor bar and pull out a bottle of mineral water. "Want one?"

"Nah, man," he says as he sits on the couch and tosses the paper down beside his thigh.

Twisting the cap off the bottle, I take a small sip as I observe JT sitting there, looking at me with clear and regretful eyes. I'm not even ashamed of myself that I think this is part of an act because he knows he's passed the point of no return with me. At this moment, he's going to do some hard-core scrambling to save himself.

I walk over to the chair that sits opposite of him, remembering all too clearly sitting here a little over six months ago looking at a woman who had been roughed up by JT. It appears I prevented that from happening again last night, but how many didn't I save?

Now the shame hits me and I square my shoulders with resolve. "This ends today, JT."

I brace, wait for him to go ballistic, but he merely nods in understanding. In a calm, assured voice, he says, "You're right. It ends today."

I blink in disbelief, but my defenses come snapping quickly back into place. "Tell me what you mean by that."

"It means I've got to get myself under control. I've forgotten how to be a businessman and have gotten sucked into the celebrity of all of this shit. The partying . . . the women . . . the drugs and booze . . . it's not who I really am. I got off track and now I'm ready to get back on track."

Well shit. I didn't expect this. I had sort of hoped that with the incriminating evidence of last night, I'd have the upper hand on JT and could use it to force him out. I figured he'd never admit to any wrongdoing, try to assure me that I was overreacting, and then we'd have a massive fight about the company.

I'm not fucking prepared for him to get all mature on me right now.

"I'm not sure I can trust you to do that," I tell him coldly, and once again, expect that to really piss him off.

"I get that," he says solemnly. "All I can do is ask you to give me another chance. I'm asking you to call on the years of friendship and everything we've been through. I'm asking you to consider everything we've got riding on this company, and even though I've been a complete tool for quite a while now, at least admit that when I'm on my game I'm really important to our success."

Fuck . . . all true.

My fingers involuntarily come to my temples and I rub at the headache that's forming. I wince, look up at him skeptically. "JT . . . I caught you drugging a woman last night. That's fucking against the law."

"She agreed to it," JT says quietly while pinning me with a direct stare.

I physically reel backward from his proclamation. "She what?"

"She agreed to it," he says simply and humbly. He's not gloating . . . just merely stating the fact. "We had a written agreement. It was a fantasy of hers, I guess. I can get you a copy Monday morning, but that woman wanted to wake up the next morning used and abused. She thought the aspect of not remembering what happened would be exciting. Figured she could fantasize about what might have happened."

"What the fuck?" I mutter as my eyes cut over to the glass floor-to-ceiling window overlooking the Financial District, which is quiet on this Sunday morning.

"It's true," JT says quietly, and my gaze slides back to him. "I might be a douche on most days and cross a lot of fucked-up boundaries, but you know me, Beck. I wouldn't hurt a woman like that."

Christ . . . he looks sincere. Sounds sincere too, but I also know JT is slick and charming when he wants to be. I have no clue if I'm being hoodwinked or not, and now all of my resolve to wrest the company away from him is crumbling. I make another attempt to poke at the merits of what he's telling me.

"I don't buy it," I grit out. "It's more than just what I saw last night. The drugs . . . taking advantage of the Babies . . . you fucking invested some of our money into a bad venture last quarter and we took a beating. You did that without my knowledge."

"I know," he says, his hands coming up in supplication. "All fucking bad moves on my part. But I'm telling you, Beck . . . if the choice is to get my shit together or lose out on one of my best friends and an amazing company I helped to create, I'm fucking telling you right now, no bullshit . . . I'll get it together. I'm just asking for another chance. I deserve it."

Fuck, fuck, fuck. What do you do when someone like JT with an ego the size of Mount Everest sits before you completely remorseful, accepting responsibility, and practically begging for another chance? A feeling of desperation overtakes me, equal parts wanting to believe in him and regain the sanctity of our business relationship—possibly our friendship—and at the same time wanting to cut ties with someone who I believe ultimately could be my downfall.

While my brain works out its inner turmoil, I wonder briefly what Sela would have me do. I know she dislikes JT intensely, and while we didn't talk about it last night—hello, too busy fucking—I know she was beyond disgusted with him. Will she think poorly of me if I don't cut him loose? Will she believe my morals are as compromised as his?

Should I even care what she thinks?

Fuck yeah, I should. I'm starting to care more and more for all things Sela Halstead, and the mere fact she's taking up residence in my thought process in making a business decision sort of says it all, right?

"Beck," JT says with soft emotion, and my eyes raise up to meet his. "I do not want to fight you for this company. I know you've had a lawyer look at things and I'm sure you know . . . unless I'm doing something illegal in the running of the business, it's going to be a fight you won't win. So I'm begging you . . . let's work this out. Let's get back on track and be a team again. I swear to you I'll get my shit together and we'll make this company even more fucking phenomenal than it already is."

I fight against it, but my shoulders sag the minute the words leave his mouth. Regardless the head of steam I came in with, he's managed to cut my legs out from underneath me with a well-planned, one-two-three-combo punch.

One, he did not illegally drug that woman last night. She apparently agreed to it.

Two, he is promising to get back on track with our business.

Three, he's reminded me that I can't take the company away from him and I'll still have to walk if I want out.

More than that, I can't overlook the years of friendship we have between us. I can't discount the tremendously deep ties we have, even if he has no clue just how important they are to me.

"I'm not sure I trust in your ability to grow the fuck up," I tell JT truthfully.

He gives an understanding laugh and nods at me. "I get it. Just give me the chance."

Sighing, I lean forward in the chair. "I'd like to request that you get my approval before any other major financial decisions are made."

"Done," he says with an earnest smile.

"And I want to see that agreement."

"Done."

And Christ . . . it looks like my hopes of coming out the victor after the meeting today have completely splintered.

"All right," I say with resignation and sudden longing to get back to the condo and sink myself into Sela. "I'll give you a shot. But this is the one and only shot I'll give."

"I won't let you down," he says, and leans forward on the

couch, extending his hand to me. I reach across and take it, a firm handshake of renewed promise occurring between us.

When we release, I stand up. "I need to get going."

"Big plans with your girl today?" JT asks, pushing up from his seat with a knowing tone that causes me to go immediately back on the defensive.

"My girl?" I ask, playing stupid. While I'm not embarrassed or shy about the fact I've asked Sela to move in with me, for some reason I don't want JT knowing this. I'm guessing it has to do with his lewd interest in her last Wednesday when she came to the office.

"Yeah . . . Sela . . . wasn't that her name?" he says offhandedly as we move toward my office door. "I saw you with her last night at the party. You two looked cozy."

"Yeah, Sela," I say vaguely without offering anything more as we walk out my door. I'm silent as I close it behind us and lock it.

"Dude . . . is she a Sugar Baby or what?" JT asks with a playful punch to my shoulder. His grin is open, not mocking at all. It seems like the old JT . . . the one I used to know way back when.

"No, she's not a Sugar Baby," I snap at him, but then decide if I'm going to give him a chance, I've got to truly give it to him. "But she has moved in with me."

JT whistles low through his teeth and gives an amused shake of his head that isn't mocking, but seemingly genuinely pleased for me. "Beck North . . . falling to commitment and monogamy. Never thought I'd see the day."

"Yeah, well . . . it's still early on. I might not even know what the fuck I'm doing, but I'm going for it."

We turn to walk down the hall toward the lobby. JT puts a hand on my shoulder and gives me a hard squeeze. "I'm happy for you, bro. You deserve a good woman, and she seems like the type that would suit you."

"She's great," I admit, surprised by how nice it feels to talk about her with someone. Even JT, who just as recently as last week came on to her right in front of me, the fucker.

"Maybe we should all do dinner one night together," JT suggests. "This is pretty epic that you have a girlfriend. Isn't this like your first ever?"

Girlfriend?

Sela Halstead . . . my girlfriend?

I hadn't thought of her like that before. Not until the word came out of JT's mouth and it didn't sound disgusting, but rather felt kind of right.

Yes . . . I have a girlfriend, and JT is right about that. First one ever.

I'm fucking twenty-eight years old and I have a girlfriend.

I give a bemused shake of my head and JT and I exit the building together. We part ways as he gets into a cab and I head toward the Millennium, intent on walking back the six blocks so I can continue to ponder everything that happened this morning.

CHAPTER 17

Sela

I don't hear the condo door open, but I do hear the jangle and clank of Beck's keys as he tosses them onto the foyer table. I stay on my side, facing the windows overlooking the Financial District, and wait for him to come to me. I woke up about twenty minutes ago and was content to stay under the warm covers and consider how drastically my life seems to be changing on an almost daily basis.

I am now somehow involved in a relationship with a man I targeted as an unwitting pawn in a scheme to commit murder.

Beck North started out as a means to an end, most likely an innocent bystander, and I sacrificed what few remaining principles I had in order to bring him deeper into my web. And yet, as I lie here and stare out the window, envisioning the gorgeous man walking down the hallway to me at this very moment, I can't help but feel that perhaps I'm the one who's trapped in a web at this moment.

I can't help feeling that's not a bad thing.

Cool air hits my naked backside, then to my surprise, an equally naked Beck slides into the bed and presses in against me, his chest to my back, his arm around my waist, his pelvis and hardening dick to my butt, and his legs tangling with mine. He pulls me in deeper and rests his chin on my shoulder.

"Did I wake you up?" he asks softly, sliding his hand up to cup my breast. He does nothing more than press his warm palm to my skin and hold it in a gentle cradle.

I shake my head. "I've been up for a little bit."

"How do you feel?" he asks tentatively.

"Very well used," I tell him on a light laugh, and then after a slight hesitation, I offer an honest admission. "Fantastic actually."

A low chuckle rumbles against me and he squeezes me closer. "Me too."

Both of us . . . reveling in the newness of what we agreed to enter into last night. Me, right this moment, amazed at how good it feels to have him wrapped around me.

Me . . . Sela Halstead . . . perhaps no longer a victim? Perhaps becoming a normal woman who enjoys intimacy?

Craves it actually . . . with this man, that is.

Amazing.

"How did it go?" I ask him, and thus I've opened us up to have a discussion about his business. But I figured, what the hell . . . we are now in a relationship, so why not. Besides . . . all starry-eyed romantic notions aside, I still need intel on JT, and this is the best way to get it.

"I think we worked things out," he says after a moment's hesitation.

"How so?" I ask, feeling a little out of sorts. Beck sounds far too calm.

"JT's promised to get his shit together. It seemed genuine—"

I spin in the bed, flopping over onto my side to face Beck. I'm outraged for a blinding second and my hands come to press on his chest to push him back from me so I can look him directly in the eye. "He tried to drug a woman last night," I grit out, my blood raging with fury.

Beck shakes his head and his hands come to cover mine with a reassuring squeeze. "That's what I thought too, Sela. I was prepared to force him to leave with that, and if he refused, I was calling the police."

"So why isn't that asshole sitting in the back of a police car right now?" I ask sarcastically.

"Because the woman agreed to it," Beck says with what I admit is a clear sound of disgust. "There's a written agreement."

I rear backward and my eyebrows shoot to the middle of my forehead before coming back down in a narrowed gaze of suspicion. "Agreed to it?"

"It was a fantasy of hers apparently," Beck says with a sheepish shrug.

"Or of his," I retort, but then immediately ask, "Did you see the agreement?"

He shakes his head. "He'll get it to me tomorrow."

I drop my eyes, look at his hands gripping mine against his chest. "I don't believe it. I don't trust him."

Beck pulls a hand from mine, puts his knuckles under my chin, and raises my gaze back to his. "Hey . . . I get you're upset about what he did, but if there's an agreement and that was consensual, I can't do anything about it."

"It wasn't consensual," I say bitterly, and pull away from him, rolling the opposite way toward the edge of the bed. Why can't he see Jonathon Townsend for what he really is?

"Hey," Beck exclaims, and his arm is wrapping around my waist, pulling me back. He comes to his knees, drags me back into him, and brings both arms around to hold me tight. His chin goes back to my shoulder and he asks softly, "What's this all about?"

I shrug.

"Sela . . . talk to me," he demands.

"There's something wrong with him," I whisper, my voice clogging with emotion. I want so badly to tell Beck exactly what I mean by that, but I can't tell him the truth yet. To do that would be to expose my intentions. Beck would see immediately that he was targeted and he would question my feelings for him. I can't do that. I can't give him up, nor the close positioning that a relationship with Beck puts me in with JT.

"He's wayward," Beck agrees with frustration. "A douche. Irrational, impulsive, and immature. He's all of that, but he's promised to get his shit together, Sela, and outside of some clear wrongdoing on his part with regard to the company, I don't have much choice but to go along with it. The only chance I had to break free was the threat of exposing him to the police last night, but that's not an option now."

I sag back against Beck, completely exhausted over this conversation. I hear it in Beck's voice . . . he's torn between wanting to get away from a bad situation and the hope that comes with promises of something better. It's certainly an easier fix, and I try desperately to give credence to Beck's thought process.

In his mind, he has nothing concrete to use against JT. He's backed into a corner and he can either walk or hope for a peaceful resolution with a bit more patience on his part. Is it wrong that he's choosing this option versus leaving his dream behind?

I don't think I can find fault with that, and while I know deep in my gut that JT was planning to drug and rape that woman last night, and I don't believe for a moment that there's a legitimate agreement in place whereby that woman agreed to that, I have to be careful about how strong my opposition is at this point. I can never underestimate not only the bonds of a long-lasting friendship between those men, but the fact that Beck and JT are intertwined by a lot of fucking money that might be more important to Beck than how great a fuck I am.

I sigh, sink further into Beck, and lean my head back so it rests on his shoulder. "I'm sorry," I mutter. "I just don't like your partner, but I totally get where you're coming from."

"Sela," Beck murmurs, sounding frustrated and exhausted all at once. "This is my only option at this moment. It doesn't mean I trust him fully and doesn't mean that he won't fuck this up. It's just the only play I have."

I nod and bring my arms up and over his, holding him tighter to me. "I know. I understand."

Beck sighs in relief and then places his teeth at my earlobe. He gives a playful bite, then licks before he says, "JT wants to do dinner with us both. He seems happy for me."

I tense up but try to sound inquisitively relaxed when I ask, "Oh yeah? You told him about us?"

"I did," Beck says, sounding happy with himself. "JT called you my girlfriend. Sounds sort of high schoolish, doesn't it?"

There's no helping the laugh that comes out of my mouth, because it does sound a little immature. I can't help jumping off track from my concerns when I ask, "So . . . is this like official or something? We're, what . . . dating?"

"Dating, fucking, cohabitating," Beck says as he pulls me down to the bed. He rolls, and I go to my back, then he rolls right on top of me. My legs spread on their own accord and he settles in between them. I love the way the hairs on his legs brush against my smooth skin and the warmth of his cock that's semihard and nestled against my bare mound. "I'm not sure what label you and I have at this point, but I'm liking where we are right at this moment."

My eyes flutter closed and I moan as he presses his pelvis down and rotates his hips a bit. "Mmmmmm . . . me too."

"Sela?" Beck says softly, and my eyes open slowly to look at him. His face is hovering over mine and his gaze is sparkling with intensity. "Do you trust me? I mean . . . at least in the way I'm handling JT right now?"

"Well, that's not for me to say," I offer hesitantly.

"Yes, it is," he admonishes me with a stern look. "You don't like him. Your run-ins with him have been less than stellar, and so you have very good reason not to like him. And while you and I haven't known each other long, I think we're both trying to build something here, and I don't want my personal or business decisions causing you to doubt me."

I blink in surprise at the desperation in his voice. I raise a hand, place it to his cheek, and realize with utter honesty that while I may not like what JT is doing to Beck, I do in fact trust what Beck's decided to do in that regard. I, better than anyone, know that sometimes you have to go with the long-range plan when it comes to dealing with snakes like Jonathon Townsend.

I nod. "Yes. I trust what you're doing with JT."

Relief swells within Beck's blue eyes and he smiles at me in gratitude. His face drops closer and his lips brush against me briefly before his forehead drops to mine. He holds still there for a moment, and I close my eyes, relishing this softly intimate embrace of silence.

"Sela?" Beck whispers my name again and then he pulls his face away. Looking down at me with the most serious expression I've ever seen on his beautiful face, he asks, "Would you trust me to let me fuck you without a condom?"

My entire body tightens with shock over his proposition and then clenches even harder with the sinful wonder of what that would feel like. I then flush warm, not from the erotic suggestion, but from the care and trust that this implies. I think I feel the stone of my heart actually start to disintegrate, collapsing in wispy, dusty piles at the bottom of my chest.

I open my mouth to answer him, but he's apparently not done. He kisses me hard, then speaks to me in urgent whispers. "You see, because here's the thing . . . I'm closer to you right now than any woman in my life outside of my sister, and that's a different kind of closeness. But I want to be even closer to you. I want to crawl inside of you, Sela, and feel every inch of you against me. I don't want any barriers and I don't want any fucking walls between us. Just you and me, touching . . . you melding into me, me into you. I want to know what that feels like with you . . . the bare skin of my cock slippery from your juices. I want to come deep inside you, planted to the root. Mark you as mine. I want that so fucking bad. Is there enough trust between us we can have that? Would you give that to me?"

My head spins and my chest constricts with aching pleasure over his words. The lust wrapped with infinite tenderness and yearning. His eyes begging me for something I've never given another man. Never wanted that closeness. Always wanted that thin barrier of rubber protecting me not just from STDs but from a true connection.

But so help me God . . . I want it now with this man.

He knows I'm protected from pregnancy because he's well aware of the packet of birth control pills that sits out in the open on his bathroom vanity. He even reminds me each morning to take it, but I've never failed in that responsibility. I think by the mere fact he's asking if I trust him must imply he trusts me, but I need to make sure.

I'm pretty sure that on my sixteenth birthday, my rapists used condoms. That's a thought that's always increased my humiliation, because they didn't wear them out of any concern for me.

They did it without knowing I was a virgin, had never had sex before, and just assumed that perhaps I was filthy and would give them something. Let's face it . . . I'm pretty sure I gave them that impression.

I also remember, in my nightmares, which I think are actual memories, the distinctive sound of a rubber snapping off just before he came in my mouth. I didn't know what that sound was then, but when the doctors found trace lubricant from condoms in my vagina and anus, it pretty much confirmed that they all covered up to protect themselves, not me. In addition, I was tested for every STD known to man, as well as given the morning-after pill as a precaution, and I came away from that experience with filth on my soul but not in my vagina.

"I'm clean," I say, my voice rough with emotion of why I can say that. I've never been with a man unprotected. Ever, and it's nice I can give that assurance to Beck.

"I know," he says, and while he's not saying he knows from actual knowledge, he's saying he knows to trust me. "You have nothing to worry about me. I promise you're safe."

"I know," I murmur the same words back to him. Same as him, I just know. That means I trust that Beck will not hurt me.

The effect on Beck is immediate. I feel his dick swell and beat against me. He closes his eyes, he takes in a deep breath, and when he opens them again, he says, "Christ . . . I want this so bad."

My answer is to spread my legs, raise my knees, and cradle him closer into me. I can feel wetness seeping out, my body more than ready to take this to the next level. Beck bends his head, places his mouth against mine, and breathes into me. He rotates his hips, and as if our bodies recognize exactly where they are supposed to be, the head of his cock presses into my opening. Beck thrusts against me gently, pushing in and working out in short, slow movements, and the feeling is exquisite. He feels so much warmer, the heat of his bare skin sliding against mine.

My pulse fires out of control over the emotion and intimacy of this moment. It's the first time I've taken a man inside of me with absolutely no barriers between our bodies, but more important . . . with nothing between our souls. We are as naked as we will ever be, bared and stripped to nothing but our basic need for each other.

"Beck," I murmur as he pushes in deeper. My legs press in hard against his ribs, I tilt my hips, and try to drag him in further.

A huge breath gusts out of his mouth, flutters across my face. He rotates his hips . . . slides deeper into me.

"Jesus," he groans almost as if he's in pain. "Nothing should feel this good, Sela. Do you know how dangerous it is to both of us to feel this good?"

My arms loop over his shoulders, circle around his neck, and I pull him to me. His chest mashes against my breasts, his cheek touches mine. "No going back now," I murmur.

Beck lifts his head . . . peers down at me with his brow furrowed. His tongue comes out, licks at his lower lip, and with a sharp punch of his hips, he slams all the way in. My neck arches and I suck in breath.

Oh my God. Holy God.

I almost burst apart as my pussy melts around him, settles in, and hugs him deep. My heart stutters . . . seizes up and then almost expands in a sigh of relief.

Beck stays completely still inside of me. He breathes in deeply, closes his eyes for a moment, and when he opens them up again, he gives me a sheepish grin. "I'm afraid to move. Afraid I might embarrass myself and blow my load in about two nanoseconds."

I giggle. Pretty sure it's the one and only time in my life I've ever done something so girlie. Beck laughs huskily and kisses me hard. He doesn't move an inch from his waist down but just kisses me deeply with thorough possession. When he pulls away, he tentatively circles his hips, grinding into me.

"Fuck," Beck mutters, and drops his forehead to mine again. "Yup . . . not going to last long."

My hands go into his hair and I massage his scalp, incredibly touched and turned on over his reaction to me.

To the woman that his friend and business partner had made untouchable for so long.

"Beck?" I tug on his hair, pull his face away from mine.

He moves reluctantly and looks down at me with that same abashed look. I tilt my hips, clench my internal muscles around his dick, and then rub my thumbs into his scalp.

"Let go," I command him softly. "Fuck me hard and come as fast as you want."

"Don't want to leave you behind," he mutters.

"I'm not going anywhere," I assure him, relax, and clench my muscles again.

His jaw locks tight, his eyes go molten, and he pushes his torso up off me. I loosen my hold around his neck and Beck shifts with a grunt as his hands come to the backs of my thighs. He pushes my legs up, spreads them wide, and then uses leverage against them to pull his hips back and slam forward again.

I'm amazed at the pure pleasure that morphs his face from a man who's infinitely gorgeous to a creature who takes my breath away. So goddamned beautiful.

"Hang on," he says tightly, and then he starts to fuck me like I've never been fucked before.

He called it right.

He doesn't last long, and although I'm more turned on than I ever have been in my entire life, the pleasure for him is too much to bear and he pulls away from me in a race to the finish. He grunts with every thrust, squeezes his eyes shut, and then mutters, "I'm sorry, Sela" before he presses in deep and releases hot within me.

Beck's body visibly shudders, the muscles in his neck and shoulders tightening in ecstasy, and then he throws his head back with a long groan of relief.

And it is without a doubt the most sensually beautiful thing I've ever seen in my life. I watch him in fascination, for the first time understanding just how stunning this experience is to me. I want to freeze this moment, the way he looks right now, and commit it to the forefront of my eternal memory.

Beck opens his eyes, stares directly at me, and lets out a huff of breath. Then his eyes narrow as his teeth bite down on his lower lip. Resolve, lust, and determination in such infinite measure burn straight through me.

"Your turn now," he says, and quickly pulls out of me. He scrambles backward, spreads my legs, and flops to the mattress. In one fluid move, his face drops and his mouth latches on to my pussy. His tongue presses against my clit and he licks at me roughly.

My hands slap in surprised pleasure to the sides of his head, and while I feel his semen leaking out of me, Beck proceeds to bring me to a massively quick and powerful orgasm that has me screaming out his name.

CHAPTER 18

Beck

Oh man . . . could she be any more adorable right at this moment?

And sexy?

Yes, Sela with her hands buried deep in a turkey's ass is a complete turn-on to me. This is so because she has no idea what she's doing but she's dedicated to the mission. Her brows are furrowed as she leans to the side of the turkey roaster and peers down at her smartphone that's sitting on the counter, checking the instructions for about the fifth time. Her tongue sticks out the side of her mouth as she contemplates the instructions versus her actions.

Her gaze goes from phone to turkey, back again to the phone. She continues pushing stuffing into the cavity with precise effort.

Her dedication to the job reminds me of last night and the filthy things we did.

Utterly fucking filthy.

While fucking Sela without barriers has now become possibly my favorite thing in the world to do, I changed it up on her last night as we made our way into bed. It had been a long day and we were tired. We had cleaned the condo and went grocery shopping for our Thanksgiving Day meal. Sela spent most of the early evening planning everything out, pulling up instructions, and setting out ingredients in tiny clusters all over the kitchen. She insisted on making the pies last night while I watched TV, and finally I had to pull her out of the kitchen when she suggested perhaps peeling the potatoes before going to bed. I'd waited enough for her and was horny as hell.

Plus . . . I had bought some toys and I wanted to experiment.

I pulled Sela into our bedroom and told her to get undressed. She did so without question and crawled onto the bed while I went into the bathroom and retrieved my bag of goodies from underneath the sink. I unceremoniously dumped them onto the mattress beside her and told her to take her pick.

She eyeballed them suspiciously, running her finger over the nine-inch dildo, the butterfly vibrator, the bottle of lube, and finally the small butt plug I thought to start her with at some point. Her eyes slid to mine as her hand rested on the vibrator.

"That your choice?" I asked in a husky voice.

She nodded and picked it up, handing it to me.

I shook my head and backed away from the bed. "Use it."

"To do what?" she asked innocently, and that made me want to jump on her and kiss her with joyous abandon that she could still be that naïve with me.

"To get yourself off," I said as I lowered myself into an armchair in the corner of the room. My dick was already hard and I rubbed it through the material of my khaki cargos.

Sela sucked in a lungful of air and let it out slowly. "While you watch?"

"Oh yeah," I told her with a sly grin. "I'm going to watch."

And what a show she put on for me. There was only a slight

hesitation as she twisted the base of the vibrator and let it hum in her hand. It was bright pink with a three-inch thin appendage with a flared head, and a soft rubber butterfly at the base.

Her eyes raised to mine and she gave me a game smile. Then she put that wicked thing between her legs, her tongue sticking out the side of her mouth in concentration, exactly the way it is now as she stuffs the turkey. Sela worked herself slowly, making tiny moans and circling her hips. She pressed the vibrator deep into her pussy, pressed the butterfly to her clit, and mewed like a starved kitten. Even though I swore to myself I'd only watch, it didn't take thirty seconds before I had my cock out and started stroking it.

It took her a while to come, and that inflated my ego that I can get her off faster. But it was beautiful and sublime, and by the time she'd reached her climax, I was strangling the base of my dick so I wouldn't unload in my hand.

I stood up from the chair, intent on walking to the bed, pulling my pants down just past my hips, and fucking her fast. But she held her hand up and stopped me. Grabbing the lube, which was strawberry flavored, she motioned to the bed and said, "Lie down."

So I did.

She squirted sweet-smelling liquid on me that coated my cock, ran over my balls in warm streams, and dribbled down the crack of my ass. It progressively got hotter as she jacked my cock for a while, and then sucked me deep into her mouth. With my eyes shut and my fingers clutching the bedspread as if my life depended on it, Sela worked me with her mouth and groaned out her own approval of the experience.

And then she got filthy with me.

With my dick stroking her tonsils and her one hand twisting me at the base, Sela snuck her other hand in between my legs, and with swift precision pressed a finger into my ass. My eyes flew open and my hips flew off the bed, causing her finger to sink deeper.

My head snapped up and I practically glared down at her, never having had a woman have the sexual proclivity to do that to me. I didn't feel violated, but I felt invaded.

She pulled her mouth off my cock, grinned at me slyly, and crooked her finger inside my body. She pressed in, stroked something that caused fire to shoot through my balls, and I shouted her name in a crazy, strangled cry of need.

Sela laughed in that sexy, smoky voice and pulled her finger back.

Pushed it back in.

Curled that finger and pressed again.

My cock jumped in her hand, and an orgasm started to bubble.

"What the fuck?" I asked her in amazement. "Where did you learn to do that, dirty girl?"

"I read about it in a book," she said impishly, her finger going still within me. "It's supposed to make you come really hard. Want me to stop?"

"Fuck no," I groaned in abandon, and then I told her, "but get your mouth back on me."

So she did. She sucked me in deep, fucked my ass with her finger, and within about thirty seconds I came harder than I ever have in my life before. I seriously almost passed the fuck out, and even as I was still squirting in her mouth, I wondered when she'd do it to me again.

It seemed my Sela was getting brave and adventurous, and I realized that she and I wouldn't have any boundaries that couldn't be crossed.

Sela continues to stuff the turkey and I reach down and adjust my stiff dick to the side of my zipper, my balls tingling from the memory of last night. I try to put that out of my head because I know she's stressed about not only getting the meal ready, but Caroline and Ally coming to visit. They should be here in a few hours and Sela's been fretting with nervousness.

"Need any help?" I ask as I walk up behind her. I take her by the hips, lean in, and kiss the back of her head.

"No," she says, her voice tight with tension. "I just need to get this in the oven and . . . fuck!"

"What?" I ask, pulling away from her as she pulls her hands out of the stuffed turkey.

"I forgot to preheat the oven," she mutters with a defeated sigh, holding her hands up and away, coated with butter and gooey stuffing.

"Relax, baby," I say as I turn to the double-oven unit built in beside the gas-top stove. "What's it need to be set to?"

Sela leans over, checks the instructions on her phone, and says, "Three twenty-five."

I turn the knob, listening to the clicking of the gas pilot, and then the subtle whoosh as it catches. I then set the temperature.

When I turn back to Sela, she stares at me with utter worry on that beautiful face. I smile at her as I put my hands back on her hips. "Relax. It's going to all be fine. What else do you need help with?"

She pulls away from me, rests her hands on the handles of the roaster, and drops her head. With a deep sigh she whispers, "I don't want to screw anything up."

My arms go around her waist and I step into her back. Resting my chin on her shoulder, I assure her, "You aren't going to screw anything up. And if you do, everyone will find it to be utterly charming and then we'll go out to dinner somewhere."

"Beck," she growls with frustration, and tries to shrug out of my grip. "This is serious. I want your sister to like me."

I squeeze her tighter. "Sela . . . darling . . . my sister is not going to be won over by the delectability of your turkey. She's going to judge you solely on the width of my smile, and trust me, your turkey doesn't make me smile any bigger. Take the pack off and relax."

She sighs again and her shoulders sag.

"You know what you need?" I ask her quietly.

"What?"

"You need an orgasm. That will relax you."

"I totally don't need that," she says, and tries to pull away from me, but she has nowhere to go. The counter prevents her flight. "I don't have time for that."

"You've got at least ten minutes before that oven gets hot enough," I argue as my hands drop to the button of her jeans. I pop it and tug her zipper down. "Plenty of time."

"Beck," she admonishes me weakly, but then my hand is diving into her panties and my fingers press against her clit. She sighs and murmurs my name again, this time in capitulation.

"Just hang on to that turkey, baby. I'll have you feeling better in no time."

The doorbell rings and Sela slams the oven door shut. She'd just basted the turkey and I have to say . . . it looks fucking fantastic. Smells even better. Her face is slightly flushed and her eyes are bright with a combination of excitement and nerves. She smooths her hands down over the dark gray wool skirt she put on. She paired it with black tights, a black turtleneck, and a pair of shiny black loafers. Her hair is tied at the back of her neck in a sleek ponytail and she looks like a young prep school girl. It's really hot, actually.

"How do I look?" she asks breathlessly.

My eyes slide down and then up again. "Most beautiful thing I've ever seen."

Her cheeks redden and her eyes lower shyly as her lips tip upward. Fucking even more beautiful.

Before I can embarrass her further, I turn and walk into the foyer. I unlock the door and pull it open.

A tiny blond-haired, brown-eyed dynamo slams into my legs, arms wrapping around tight. "Uncle Beck."

I reach down, pick Ally up, and give her a quick hug before sitting her on my hip. Caroline steps over the threshold and I hold my free arm out. She steps into a tight hug, her arms going around my waist.

"Hey, sis," I say as I press a kiss on her hair, the same color as mine. She pulls back and grins up at me with blue eyes that also match mine.

"Oh, you look great. A sight for our sore eyes," she gushes, patting me hard on my lower back. Her gaze slides past my shoulder and her smile gets brighter. She pulls away and steps past me. I turn to follow and watch as she walks up to Sela, who's standing there with her hands clutched in nervousness before her.

"And you must be Sela," Caroline says in wide-eyed wonder. She steps forward, and Sela hesitantly extends her hand. Caroline ignores it and wraps Sela up in a hug. "Oh my God . . . Beck emailed me a picture of you but it didn't do you justice."

I roll my eyes and hitch Ally up on my hip a little higher. "Okay, that's enough Caroline. You're ruining my street cred."

Caroline ignores me and turns Sela toward the kitchen. "The turkey smells wonderful. Let me help you finish whatever up. Beck can entertain Ally and we can talk. You have wine, right?"

"Um, yeah . . . actually we do," Sela says with a return smile, and they both walk off, leaving me behind.

I hear them murmuring in excited undertones, Caroline beside herself that her big brother has actually got a girlfriend, and Sela clearly relieved to finally understand what I'd been telling her. That my sister is cool as hell.

Craning my head, I look at Ally. "Want to go watch some TV?"

She cocks an adorable four-year-old eyebrow that descended directly from her mom's DNA. *"Dora the Explorer?"*

"I was thinking football," I counter.

"Dora," she says adamantly.

I sigh and tickle at her ribs. She giggles and wraps her arms around my neck. "Fine, you little monster. Dora it is."

I carry Ally into the living room, sneaking a peek into the kitchen. Sela is uncorking a bottle of wine, and Caroline is pulling glasses out of a cabinet. The smell of roasting turkey makes my stomach rumble, and the knowledge that I'm getting ready to have a unique family holiday causes warmth to spread through my chest.

It's a fucking fantastic feeling that I could most definitely get used to.

CHAPTER 19

Sela

"Are you sure you don't want to come with us?" Beck asks as he pulls a sweatshirt over his head. I watch as his head pokes through the top, messing his hair up. He threads his arms through and tugs the bottom down. So simple and so sexy. He runs his fingers through his mop, perhaps making it messier and even sexier, and I have to restrain myself from launching myself at him.

I seem to want to perpetually do that.

"No, I'm going to stay here and give you quality time with Caroline and Ally," I tell him firmly. "They're leaving tomorrow and I want you to have some alone time."

Beck steps into me, wraps his arms around my waist, and pulls me into his body. I tilt my face up, oh so naturally to accept his lips, and he leans down. A soft kiss and a smile. "You know the time would be more quality if you came with us."

"Nice try, Mr. North," I tell him as I pull out of his embrace before I'm tempted. "But I'm staying and you're going. And you're not going to change my mind."

I really do want him to change my mind, but I also think he needs this time with his sister and niece. They've been here only twenty-four hours, but I've seen enough to know that they are incredibly close as siblings and that they don't get to see each other enough.

I'm not quite sure why though. Caroline and Ally live north in Healdsburg, only about an hour and a half away, but as far as I can tell, they only really see each other at holidays. Beck told me last night as we lay in bed together that Caroline hates the city and Beck is always so busy he just has a hard time getting away. It was with a bit of sadness and shame that he said, "Work just gets in the way sometimes."

I snuggled in closer to him, distressed on his behalf over things he's missing out on.

Then he added, "And I'm starting to realize that work might not be the most important thing."

That prompted me to kiss him.

That prompted him to roll me on to my back, whereby he plunged into me swiftly. He rocked against me slowly, keeping his mouth on mine the entire time to swallow my cries so Caroline and Ally couldn't hear us. God, it was fantastic, the way we just undulated against each other, barely moving, yet I felt him everywhere. It took a while for us both to build up to climax, and then the coup de grâce of all perfect fucking happened. We had simultaneous orgasms that caused us to shudder and gasp in surprise.

I was so overwhelmed I murmured into his chest, "Beck . . . it's never been like this. Ever."

"I know," was all he said in return.

We fell asleep in that position and stayed wrapped tight against each other all night.

"Okay," Beck says as he pulls away from me. "We're going to head over to the Ferry Building and poke around for a while. Maybe grab some lunch. If you change your mind, just call me and I'll let you know where we are."

I follow Beck out of our bedroom—so weird . . . thinking of it as "our" bedroom, but that's what Beck calls it, so I'm going with it. I'm not sure when I'll actually consider this my home. My lease isn't up on my apartment until next summer, but Beck has covered those expenses so I'm not worrying about it just now.

Caroline and Ally are waiting in the living room. They look at Beck expectantly.

"Any luck?" Caroline asks as her eyes flick from Beck to me.

Beck shakes his head. "Nope. She insists we need alone time together."

My mind is nearly changed when Ally pushes away from her mom and runs up to me. "Come with us, Sela. Mommy says she wants to see you and Uncle Beck holding hands and making out in public."

"Oh geez," Caroline says with a red face. "That was a secret, Ally."

I laugh and ruffle Ally's yellow hair. She looks nothing like Caroline and I'm assuming everything like her father. When I asked Beck about the nonexistent man, he said tersely, "He's not in the picture at all. Ally doesn't even know him."

By his tone of voice, I could tell it wasn't a good situation and thus I dropped the subject quickly.

"All right," Beck says as he leans down and kisses me on the cheek. "Be back in a little bit. Want us to bring you anything?"

My hands go to Beck's waist, and I love the way his lips linger against my skin. I shake my head. "I'm good. You guys have fun and I'll see you soon."

As soon as they get their coats and walk out the door I pull my phone out of my pocket and dial my father. I tried to call him yesterday but didn't get any answer. I didn't leave a message and frankly forgot to call him again as I was having so much fun just hanging out with Caroline and Beck. Long after Ally went to bed last night, we all stayed up drinking wine, and the North siblings regaled me with tales of growing up in a privileged world that they both seemed to detest. While Beck still lives the lifestyle he was born to, now it's a product of his hard work. My understanding is that Caroline has the same trust fund as Beck, but she lives a modest existence in Healdsburg working as an assistant to an art gallery owner. It's clear from listening to them both that they have almost no relationship with their parents.

I pull up my dad's number and tap on it. It rings twice before Maria answers pleasantly. "Hi, Sela. Happy Thanksgiving."

"Happy Thanksgiving," I tell her warmly. I normally might be a little irked at her answering for my dad, but having gone through a warm and fulfilling holiday with Beck and his little family, I'm feeling more magnanimous toward her. "Is Dad around?"

"Sure is," she says, and I hear the phone being handed off.

"Hey, baby," my dad says gruffly with emotion. While we may have drifted apart a little after Mom died, I'll never forget the strength of that dad after my rape. He became my champion and protector after that, making me feel as secure as a young girl could after having her innocence brutalized.

"Hey, Dad," I say softly as I walk into the kitchen. I open the fridge and pull out a bottle of water.

"How was your Thanksgiving?" he asks, and I hear the creak of his recliner and can imagine him cocking it back and throwing his feet up.

"It was great," I tell him. "I ate dinner with Beck, and his sister and niece joined us."

"Excellent," he says enthusiastically. "Any chance I'll get to meet this guy?"

I talk to my dad at least once a week on the phone. While I have not admitted that I'm living with Beck, I did tell him all about my new boyfriend. That first conversation was filled with a lot of "wows" and "that's awesome" from my dad, a man who I think always despaired I'd be able to open myself up to a relationship.

"One day," I say vaguely, because that all depends on where this is truly heading. While if it were only a matter of Beck and me seeking a happily ever after, that would be a no-brainer to get him over to meet my dad as soon as possible. But considering that I might be killing Beck's partner in the near future, and that might or might not lead to my incarceration, I figure I better not make him any promises.

My dad starts to chatter on about his Thanksgiving, telling me in detail about every side dish they had. Maria's son and daughter-in-law joined them, and I had to laugh when Dad whispered into the phone that Maria just hadn't mastered a pumpkin pie to rival my mom's.

I walk from the kitchen into the living room, intent on curling up on the couch, when my eyes involuntarily stray to the foyer.

To the side table sitting there.

To Beck's keys he left on that table.

He had no reason to take them, since they were walking to the Ferry Building and I was staying here.

My dad's voice fades away and I walk up to the table. I grab the key chain and turn it over in my palm to study.

In addition to his Audi key, I recognize the condo key. It has a blue rubber protector over the head, same as mine. There are two more door keys on the ring, and I know one of them belongs to his locked office. My head swivels and I gaze down the hallway.

". . . so we're just hanging here gorging on leftovers. What are you up to today?" my dad's voice cuts back into my thoughts.

I shake my head and my fingers curl around the keys. "Um . . . we're all going to hang out at the Ferry Building."

The lie comes easily, my focus intent on the hallway as I start walking that way.

"Sounds like fun," he says jovially. "Well, you just try to plan a trip home and bring that man of yours with you. I can't wait to play overprotective dad."

My father laughs heartily and I give a half chuckle, the office door looming closer. "All right, Dad. I gotta go, but I love you."

"Love you too, sweetie," he says. "Talk to you later."

"Bye," I say vaguely, and disconnect as I come to the door. I pocket my phone and hold the keys out in front of me, considering which one may fit the lock. Doesn't matter if I get it wrong. Got plenty of time to try again.

I choose a key and slip it into the keyhole. With my other hand bracing the knob, I turn my wrist and feel the lock give smoothly.

My heart rate jacks up, and a rush of adrenaline goes through me. I start to twist the knob, but then a feeling of foreboding rips through me. I hesitate a moment . . . consider my options.

This isn't optimal.

I turn the key back the opposite way, reengage the lock, and pull it free. My heart is still pounding but I feel immense relief in my decision to back away, knowing this was the right call.

I have no clue when Beck will be back. It could take me hours to search his office and I don't want to be interrupted. It has to be done on a day when he's at work and I have little to no chance of being caught.

I glance down at my watch. Beck's been gone less than ten minutes, and I'm better served by trying to rush out quickly and get a copy made; that way I can search at a more opportune time.

I tell myself firmly my hesitation has nothing to do with my distaste in betraying the man I've come to care a great deal about.

No matter what my feelings are for Beck, I simply have to do this, I reassure myself. This is for my own good, and if I have to sacrifice his trust in this small way, I'm going to have to just fucking live with it.

Besides, I reason to myself, if I can cut this albatross known as Jonathon Townsend from around my neck, I can then truly be free to be everything to Beck that he deserves. I further reason to myself that this has to be done for Beck's own good. That it's the only way I can give myself to him freely and without any walls or lies staining our relationship. Even better reasoning, if I can end JT's existence, I will be freeing Beck from a toxic relationship with his business partner.

I pocket the keys and walk quickly into the bedroom. I put on a light jacket and grab my purse. I know there's a local hardware store about four blocks away, in the opposite direction of the Ferry Building. With any luck I can be there and back within half an hour . . . no more than forty-five minutes, with a copy of the office key safely in hand.

Yeah . . . that's my best play at this moment.

The elevator comes to a halt, and I pat the copy of the key in my pocket and flip Beck's key chain jauntily in my hand. I feel good about this. I have a plan starting to come together.

The elevator doors open and I step into the hallway, Beck's condo directly ahead. I raise my head and come to a dead halt. Beck stands there with his arms crossed over his chest. Caroline's got Ally in her arms and her face is red and shiny with tears.

"What's going on?" I ask cautiously as I walk toward them.

"Ally got in a snit and pitched a toddler tantrum," Caroline says with a sheepish grin. "After a two-minute shrieking session in the bookstore, we decided to head back. Figured we could just hang here today."

My eyes cut over to Beck and he's eyeballing the key chain in my hand. "We couldn't get in."

"Oh," I say softly as I look down at the keys. "Sorry."

"Where were you?" Beck asks, and I can tell by the tone of his voice he can't fathom where I would have been with his keys. This makes me panic and my mind races to find the perfect excuse, but nothing comes to mind.

"Um," I hedge for a split second too long, because it sounds like I'm searching for a lie, so I just blurt out, "I borrowed your car. I decided to go to my apartment and pick up a few things."

It's completely obvious when Beck's jaw tightens, and I know he doesn't believe me. "Didn't make it very far, did you?"

My feet move and I walk quickly to the door, avoiding eye contact with him. I put the key in the lock and open the door. Caroline slips through, keeping her own head down. I know she can feel the tension between us.

I start to follow her in but Beck grabs my arm and turns me to him. He looks at me in question, expecting a response. I swallow hard and lift my chin in a display of a confidence I'm not feeling at all. "I made it as far as the First Street on-ramp and the traffic was horrible. Decided to come back and see if maybe you wanted to go with me later."

His eyes bore into mine, actually flicking back and forth as if he's trying to see truth in what I'm saying. He stares at me so long I almost blurt out the entire truth to him.

Everything.

About JT and my nefarious plans.

But then Beck just gives me a curt nod, drops his hand from my arm, and walks into the condo. I take a deep breath and follow him in.

Caroline is setting Ally up on the couch and has the TV remote in hand, presumably to get her favorite *Dora the Explorer* to watch. She shoots me a sympathetic smile and then her head turns to follow Beck as he walks back into the bedroom. I smile back at her and hurry down the hall after her brother, feeling impending doom rushing in on me.

When I enter the bedroom, I find him at the window looking out over the city, his back stiff and arms crossed over his chest. I close the door softly.

He turns to me and asks, "Are you lying to me?"

I force myself not to wince at the condemnation in his voice and his acute perception. "No, of course not."

God, yes, I'm lying, Beck, and I'm so very sorry. I hope you will forgive me this transgression. I swear I have good reason.

"You're lying," he says adamantly. His arms fall away from his chest and in strides up to me, taking his key chain from my hand.

"I'm not," I say quickly.

"Sela," he barks at me, and I snap my mouth shut. "When you didn't answer the door, I thought I might have an extra house key in my car. I went down to the garage to look because I have a remote concierge unlocking service through Audi. My car was there. No extra key in there, but my car was fucking there. And I know we're still trying to get to know each other, and you probably haven't figured this out yet, but I have no patience whatsoever to suffer liars in my life. I refuse to do it. So where in the fuck were you and why in the fuck are you lying to me?"

I shrink back from the anger in his voice. I practically shrivel up from the pain in his eyes.

"I went for a walk," I whisper, the need for self-preservation making the lie fall from my mouth easily. "Your keys were just lying there and were easier to take than going back to the bedroom for mine."

"Then why lie to me?" he grits out. "Why tell me you took the car to your apartment, which I don't give a shit if you use my car. I just care that you lied to me."

"I don't know," I blurt out, panicked that I may be losing something very important in this very moment. I forget about the perfect story and pour out emotions that are based in truth. I hope the half-truths cover up a full truth I could never tell him. "I went for a walk. I've been overwhelmed with everything that's going on with you and me. It seems too good to be true and I've never had this before, and I'm scared, Beck. I'm afraid it's going to all fall apart on me and I can't tell you that, because I don't want to seem clingy and unsure of myself. You like my confidence, right? So I don't want to seem anything less than that to you. And when I got off the elevator and saw you there, and you looked angry . . . I just lied. I wasn't thinking straight. But I swear . . . that's all I was doing. I was out for a walk."

Beck turns away from me in frustration, scrubs his hand through his hair. He then spins back and looks at me with sadness. "Why would you feel so unsure about me? What have I done to make you feel that way?"

I can't help the shaky sigh of relief that comes out, and I hope he doesn't understand that my relief stems from the fact that he just bought that half-baked story. I cover it up by immediately walking up to him, pressing my cheek to his chest, and wrapping my arms around his waist. I squeeze him to me, fear gripping me when he doesn't return the embrace.

My voice is small and weak when I say, "I'm sorry. I'm just so afraid of fucking things up with you and I don't want to lose this."

Then I tell him an absolute truth. "I think you're the best thing to ever happen to me, and when you're given a gift like that, the prospect of losing it can be a little consuming."

Beck lets out a pained moan and his arms wrap around my upper back. He squeezes me hard and presses his lips to the top of my head. "Jesus, Sela. I'm not going anywhere and there's not much you could do to push me away from you. You're perfect as is and I'm insanely happy being with you, okay?"

I nod into his chest. Burrow in tighter to him.

"Just don't lie to me," he says gruffly. "Don't ever lie to me, don't ever do anything to make me distrust you, and everything is golden. Okay?"

My heart sinks.

Because I fully intend to keep lying to him until my quest is complete.

CHAPTER 20

Beck

Three sharp raps to my office door have me raising my head and blinking my bleary eyes. I rub my fingers over them, happy for the break from reading code.

"Come in," I say gruffly, picking up the bottle of mineral water on my desk and taking a long swig.

The door swings open and JT walks in. He looks . . . different. Instead of the normal custom-tailored, three-thousand-dollar suit he wears with diamond cuff links, he's got on a pair of dark jeans and a burgundy cashmere sweater. He never dresses casual for the office and it catches me off guard, because JT likes to flaunt his money, and nothing says money like Armani.

I immediately notice his eyes are clear and his pupils are normal, and I wince internally that this has become my standard practice whenever I see him. He shoots me a grin and says, "What's up, bro?"

"Not much," I say, leaning back in my chair. "Just reviewing some code for the new platform. It's a bit buggy."

"I saw the mock-ups last week," he says as he sits down in one of the guest chairs opposite my desk. He props an ankle on the opposite knee and relaxes back casually. He looks almost . . . carefree.

This should make me happy, but rather makes me suspicious. I wince again, because I'm supposed to be giving him a second chance.

"Good holiday weekend?" he asks, his eyes bright with interest.

"Um . . . yeah. Caroline and Ally came to visit for a few days, and Sela and I just hung out around the city this weekend. You?"

"I spent it up at my folks' place in Windsor. Just relaxing with them. Actually had time to read a book."

JT's parents have a winery estate in the Sonoma Valley. It actually produces, but it's more of a vacation home than anything for them, and they only use it sporadically, preferring to spend most of their time at their home in Sausalito. JT's family made their money in tech but they have their fingers in several pies.

I cock an eyebrow at JT. "You just went there and relaxed? Read a book?"

"I had some wine and cheese too," he says with a wink. "And turkey, of course."

I shake my head and try not to smile at his winsome ways. I know he's trying to show me the new JT, but it seems odd to me. It's been so long since I've seen this I'm having a bit of a hard time trusting it.

"Did Karla get that agreement to you last Monday?" he asks, his expression turning serious. "You never said anything."

"Yeah, I got it."

It's sitting in my desk right now under lock and key. Karla brought a copy to me, sealed in an envelope, as soon as I walked in that Monday morning after I met with JT. I grimace in distaste at what I'd read, but if the signature on the document is real, then that Sugar Baby clearly had a seriously kinky side that she wanted JT to indulge her in.

I didn't accept the agreement on its face. I looked up the Sugar Baby on the database—Melissa Fraye—and compared her photo to the woman I remembered that night at the mixer. It was the same. I even pulled up the scanned photo of her Sugar Baby agreement with us, and the signatures matched.

That did not ease my conscience completely though. I know way too much about computers and graphics, and know exactly how easy it is to pirate a signature off one document and place it on the other. I know I shouldn't be concerned. I know I should give JT the benefit of the doubt, but I can't help but fucking remembering Sela's words and how assured she'd sounded that morning when I came back and told her about my meeting with JT.

I don't believe it.

I don't trust him.

It wasn't consensual.

Her doubt in him makes me still doubt to some degree, and I have to marvel at the way in which I seem to trust her but not a man I've known for far longer.

A man I have far many more ties and memories with than I do a woman I've known for a little less than a month. JT and I go back for years. Our parents did business together. He came to all of my ostentatious birthday parties, and I went to his. We skied together in Tahoe on winter breaks, and backpacked together in Europe. Prep school days, Stanford. Next to Caroline and Ally, he's the person I was closest to in the world.

Beyond all of that, JT and I share a bond that Sela can't comprehend and that is deeper than even what she and I will ever have.

A sudden spark of guilt hits me hard, that at some point I had forgotten that. When JT went off track, I just let myself get consumed by my career and building this business. I ignored his partying and turned my nose up at the Sugar Babies he'd burn through. I figured it was his due, I guess, and only when it got to a breaking point did I bother to take the fucking time to do something about it.

Maybe . . . just maybe if I'd paid a little bit better attention, and been a friend a little earlier, I could have pulled him back from the brink a little quicker.

"Those look like some deep thoughts, dude," JT says, and I blink my eyes, bringing him into focus. His head is tilted, looking at me with amusement.

I shake my head and give him a confident smile. "Nah . . . just still thinking about the code I was reviewing."

Not about to tell him that I'm having a hard time buying this nice-guy act.

"Remember that time you and Barry Kratzel were building that . . . what the fuck was that program . . . the one where it would measure a woman's ability to be a one-night stand?"

I snorted and then a laugh popped out. "Yeah. We thought it was brilliant. Luckily our professor did too, but I think that was only because he was recently separated from his wife and was hoping like hell it worked."

JT laughs right along with me, the laugh lines around his squinted eyes looking natural and without the calculation that I normally see. "I tried that stupid thing out and hooked up with that crazy girl in my econometrics class. Your fucking program told me I had a 99.3 percent chance of her not caring that I didn't call her the next day."

Grinning at JT, I remember that with fondness. It was a program I'd created my freshman year in a course entitled Reliable

Algorithms. I used my buds in the fraternity to beta test it. It was an app where you could be out on a date, take a piss break after you'd had some time to talk to the girl, and answer a series of ten questions based on what you'd learned so far. It would then spit out odds on her being the perfect one-night stand. We didn't really think it had much practical application outside of drunk college students, but figured it would impress our professor.

We got an A on the project.

JT banged a girl who ended up stalking him for almost a month before she finally got the hint he wasn't interested after their one night together.

"Those were the good ol' days," JT says, turning his head to look out the window with a slightly regretful tone in his voice.

"Yeah, they were," I agree softly.

JT clears his throat and stands up from the chair, turning to look back at me. "So, listen . . . I've got Sam putting together a proposal for us to consider. It's for a start-up based out of Santa Clara, and they're developing software that will read facial expressions."

"I read about that a few weeks ago," I say with a nod. "It's supposed to analyze emotional responses consumers have to certain products."

"Yeah . . . it looks very promising. I want you to take a look at it and give me your thoughts."

I blink my eyes in surprise. JT never runs this shit past me. At first I didn't care, because he's the one with the MBA and is the king of investing, but it appears he may be truly trying to forge a stronger partnership with me.

"Sure, be glad to," I say with a smile of gratitude.

"Cool," he says, and turns toward the door. When he reaches for the knob, he turns back and says, "Are you and Sela interested in getting together for dinner sometime soon? I'd like to learn more about this woman who seems to have taken you off the market."

I study his face carefully, trying to see if there is an ulterior motive. Perhaps sleazy intent. At the very least, too creepy of an interest. Instead, he looks back at me with open friendliness and I decide to finally give one to him.

"Yeah . . . that would be great," I say with a smile. "How about Saturday?"

"Perfect," JT says with a grin. "That will give me time to find a presentable date of the non–Sugar Baby variety."

"Really trying to turn over a new leaf, huh?"

God, I hope that didn't sound too shitty.

JT just laughs and nods. "I told you, bro. I'm getting my shit together, and I'm sure my mom won't have any problem finding me a nice, young socialite with a perfect pedigree for me to bring along."

"Sounds lovely," I say dryly.

"Dude . . . you know it's not, but I don't want to feel like a third wheel, so I'm going to go call my mother right now."

"Can't wait to meet the future Mrs. Jonathon Townsend," I say with a laugh.

JT grimaces and shakes his head, but there's amusement on his face. "Later," he says, and then he's gone.

I glance at my watch. Only 3:45 P.M. and I wonder what Sela's doing. Her classes don't start back up until tomorrow, so I'm thinking she's probably home all alone and needing some company. I glance back to the code, knowing I need to get this done.

Back to my watch and think of Sela.

Fuck the code. I can work on it later tonight after she falls asleep.

• • •

I flip through the mail as I walk to the condo door. A small cream envelope with my name and address written in emerald green calligraphy stares up at me. I grimace and open it, knowing what it is and yet still feeling compelled to read it.

The honor of your presence is requested to join Mr. and Mrs. Beckett W. North, Sr., as we celebrate the Christmas holiday with our friends and family . . .

Jesus. I hate getting these things.

There are two functions every year that I'm expected to make an appearance at. First is my father's birthday, which is in June, and the second is their annual Christmas party. While my relationship with my parents is tenuous at best, arcticlike cold at its worst, I do try to accommodate these functions. My father, who is an investment advisor and a very good one at that, has an immense backlist of helpful business contacts, and I'd be a fool not to take advantage of at least that opportunity.

I'm surprised when I see a handwritten note at the bottom in black ink. I recognize my mom's handwriting: *Beck . . . we look forward to seeing you soon. Perhaps encourage Caroline to attend.*

I bark out a laugh at the ludicrousness of that statement and tuck the stack of mail under my arm. I guarantee you that Caroline threw the card unopened into the trash the minute she saw the calligraphy and return address. She has no need of our father's business pull and she sure as shit has no need for her parents. They failed her when she needed them the most and she'll never forgive that.

Neither will I for that matter, but I'll probably attend anyway. I'm sure Sela would be happy to go with me, and that will make it at least tolerable.

I unlock the condo door, my blood firing at the prospect of

seeing her. It's like I can feel her presence just on the other side, and my heart races as my body tightens all over. It's a feeling I won't ever get used to, and don't ever want to anyway.

I push the door open, feel the utter silent stillness, and then my eyes immediately come to Sela as I see her sitting in an overstuffed white leather chair near the window. It normally doesn't belong there but rather flanks one side of the black marble fireplace, and she clearly dragged it over there. Her bare feet are curled up underneath of her, and her head is resting on the back of the chair with her face tilted toward the enormous wall of windows. She's staring out over the bay, and in her right hand, she loosely holds a utility knife.

She doesn't even turn to acknowledge me.

"Hey," I say as I set the mail down on the table and drop my keys on top of it. As I shut the door, she turns to look at me and her face is a blank canvas. Normally I'm greeted with a soft smile. Often she'll walk up to me, hips swaying before giving me a sweet kiss on my lower jaw.

Now she just looks at me impassively, not even surprised to see me standing there.

"Hey," she says, her voice low with a morose tinge.

"What are you doing?" I ask, my eyes dropping to the utility knife.

She looks down at it, her thumb rubbing over the plastic handle. "Nothing," she says vaguely. "I was getting ready to open up some of my boxes."

Sela and I went to her apartment on Sunday and she packed up more of her stuff to move in. It was mostly the rest of her clothing, books, and a few framed photos of her family. Three boxes in all and they sat in the corner of the living room untouched.

Something about Sela sitting there, looking sadly out the window with a box cutter in her hand seems terrifying to me. She looks small and alone, and despite the bright light pouring in, seems to be filled with darkness.

I walk over to her, skirting the couch and coffee table. When I reach the chair, I squat down in front of her, placing my hands on her thighs. She stares down at me, her face revealing nothing.

"What's wrong?" I ask.

A small smile comes to her face. She reaches her free hand out and touches the tips of her finger to my jaw before they fall away. "Nothing. Just sitting here enjoying the view."

My head turns to look out at the dark bay waters sparkling with the rays of today's unusually bright sun. I turn back to her. "You look sad," I observe.

"Pensive," she offers instead.

"About what?"

Sela shrugs. "Lots of things."

"Not helpful," I say with a small smile, and I'm heartened when she returns it.

"What are you doing home so early?" she asks, not sounding the least surprised and in a suave change of subjects. Or maybe it's just that her voice sounds dull, matching the gray that seems to be emanating from her.

"Thought I'd come spend time with you," I tell her, my thumbs stroking her legs through her denim jeans.

And suddenly, a little color comes back into the picture as she gives me a sweet smile, her head tilted to the side. She uncurls her legs, which dislodges my hands. I stand up, and she does the same, stepping into my body. She presses her cheek to my chest and wraps her arms tight around my waist.

"I'm glad," she whispers.

I squeeze her affectionately, rubbing my hand into her lower back. "What do you want to do?"

She doesn't hesitate a moment. Pulling back, she drops the utility knife to the hardwood floor where it clatters unceremoniously, and tucks her fingers underneath my belt buckle. Giving me a tug, she turns toward the hallway that leads to our bedroom.

"I want to fuck," she says simply, and who am I to deny her?

I follow her back.

CHAPTER 21

Sela

I pull off my shirt the minute I step into our room, dropping it to the floor. Beck walks over to the dresser and takes off his watch, setting it on the polished top. He then pulls his own top off, a light gray cashmere V-neck sweater that hugs him in all the right places.

My stomach tightens marginally as his back is revealed to me and I take in the red phoenix on his shoulder. I know in my heart of hearts that Beck was not there that night. Going by simple math alone, he would have been eighteen and in his last year of prep school. JT is four years older, meaning he would have been twenty-two when he raped me. That alone doesn't add up.

But more than that, I just know Beck would never have that in him. He would never hurt or violate a woman. He would never participate in a brutal gang rape. His violent reaction to JT that night he tried to drug that woman proves it, and besides . . . I just know it deep in my soul.

At least that's what I tell myself every time I see that tattoo.

I normally will drop my gaze away, wait for him to turn that beautiful chest my way before I can look upon him again. The overwhelming sadness I've been feeling the last few days seems to compound as I look upon it. He toes his shoes off. Undoes his belt.

I stare at the phoenix, hating that there's a part of Beck that I hate.

Hating it even more because I hate myself for what I'm doing to him.

Ever since last Friday when he caught me sneaking back into the condo . . . when he called me a liar, not even really understanding how deceptive I was being . . . I've been mired in guilt. During those few minutes when he called me on my lie, and I thought he was going to throw me clean from his life, I knew in my soul that Beck North was the best thing that ever happened to me. When it all seemed to be crumbling away, and I was clawing furiously to get him to see past my lies, I had a moment of clarity when I realized that revenge on JT was not ever going to be worth the hurt I could put on Beck.

Despite that horrid tattoo that seems to leer at me, a constant reminder of everything that was taken away from me, I don't think I can go through with my plans.

Today I wandered around the condo aimlessly, my copy of his office key tucked into the bottom of my makeup bag in the bathroom. It was the prime opportunity for me to search his office, and yet I steered clear of it, refusing to even look at that fucking office door.

Even if I knew without a doubt that there was a clear-cut answer in there about how I could avenge myself, I just couldn't make myself do it. I just couldn't betray Beck in that way. Even more horrific to consider was the effect it could have on him if I was successful in killing JT, especially if he ever realized that he was an unwitting partner in my murderous plot. He'd never be able to forgive himself, and I cannot bear to ever lay a torturous burden like that upon him.

And while I'd been in a funk since our near undoing last week, I sank into a dark depression today as I realized my quest to destroy my rapists was going to go unfulfilled. While in my head I knew that the reward of having Beck in a completely transparent and trusting way would be more than enough for me, I was heavily mourning my loss of vengeance. So sunk into my nasty thoughts, I had pulled the utility knife out of Beck's kitchen drawer and carried it around with me.

Did I think about using it on myself?

Not really.

But I held on to that vile thing as a reminder of how far I'd sunk before, and that at that point in my life I didn't have anything to live for.

With Beck in my life, I couldn't say that now.

So it meant that there was going to be a part of me that would always be damaged, and I would just have to live with it.

I would just have to learn to live with it.

Beck turns to face me, but the tattoo is still in my peripheral vision as his back is reflected in the mirror that sits on top of the dresser. He smiles at me, his hands pulling the belt free of its loops and dropping it to the floor.

I would just have to learn to live with it.

My eyes cut to his reflection, and I swallow hard against the bitterness and hatred within me. I walk across the room as he watches me with heavy-lidded eyes. When I reach him, I step to his side, and with my hand on his waist, I turn him gently away from me.

Lifting my hand, which is shaking with fear, I place the tips of my fingers against the left wing of the phoenix. Beck lets out a sigh as I trace the outline.

"What are you doing?" he asks gruffly. I've never once mentioned his tattoo or inquired about it. This is the first time I've ever touched it.

"Where did you get this?" I ask softly, running my fingers along his skin . . . tracing the flaming feathers on the tail.

"A little tattoo parlor in Palo Alto," he says.

"While you were at Stanford." It's a statement I can easily deduce based on the fact I assume this might be a fraternity thing and I knew JT and Beck went to Stanford together.

"That's right. Got it after I pledged."

"All members of the fraternity have it?"

"No," he says with a shake of his head. "Just a small group of us."

Bile rises in my throat over the implication but I push it down. Beck was not a part of my rape.

He wasn't.

I make myself lean forward and press my lips to the skin colored with red, gold, and orange feathers of flame. It's warm and he smells like Beck. Clean, fresh, wild.

He turns abruptly, his arms snaking around my waist. He peers down at me intently, understanding that something is going on that he just doesn't quite understand.

"Sela?" he asks in question.

"I'm sad," I tell him truthfully, thinking I should feel self-conscious over admitting a vulnerability to this man, and yet feeling completely and utterly safe in my revelation.

Beck's eyes go soft with sympathy and his hands come to my face. He cradles me gently, bends down closer, and kisses my forehead. "What's wrong, baby?"

Your best friend raped me.

While I don't think you did, I have maybe a sliver of a doubt. No, not really. I'm sorry to even think that.

I care for you more than I care about justice for myself, and that makes me miserable.

Yet I can tell him none of that. If I'm going to let it go, that means I can never burden Beck with my knowledge, my memories, or my suspicions. I need to take him as is, and let him be oblivious to my darkest days.

That will be for the best.

So I vow to myself that this will be the last time I lie to him. "I tend to get blue around the holidays. Missing my mom, I guess."

He tilts his head, his blue eyes darkening in sorrow for me. "What can I do to help?"

I shrug, but then throw out a suggestion that I'm not sure will really make anything better for me, but might make him feel like he can help. "Maybe we could put up some of her decorations for Christmas. My dad has them boxed up for me."

"Of course we can do that," he says, and then pulls me into him. I bury my face in his neck and feel his warm skin against mine as we press together. "Where are the decorations?"

"At my dad's. We'd have to go get them."

"So I get to meet your dad, huh? Is he going to like me?"

"He's going to adore you," I assure him with a smile. My dad will utterly love him.

"Like you adore me?" he asks, his voice amused, but I also know this is a serious question.

"Not as much as I adore you, but it will be close," I assure him.

Then Beck's mouth is on mine, and I know he adores me too just by the ferocity of his kiss. Maybe he can't say it in words, but that's okay with me. I can read enough into his actions to know that Beck is on the same page as I am.

His hands come to the back of my bra and he flicks it open before pulling it from me. Then he's opening my jeans, pushing them down my hips and dropping to his knees before me. Fingers going under the elastic of my panties, he pulls them down enough to gain access and runs his tongue up my center. My knees threaten to buckle, but I'm saved when he wraps his arms around them, picks me up, and turns to deposit me on the bed.

In moments, he has the rest of our clothing off and he's climbing onto the mattress. I part my legs, welcome him against me. He lays his body flush against mine and kisses me, hands roaming up my rib cage, his cock swelling against my pelvis.

"You're so goddamn beautiful, Sela. Inside and out," he says, tracing a path with his lips down my neck, over my collarbone. His body inches down mine, blazing fiery trails of warm kisses over my breasts, down my stomach. With his hands to the backs of my thighs, he lifts my legs and brings them over his shoulders.

Beck's fingers dive into me as he gives my pussy a hot, wet, openmouthed kiss that sends shock waves of pleasure zinging through my body.

"Taste so goddamn good too," he mutters in between licks and sucks.

My neck arches and my hands go into his soft hair. "Beck."

"That's right," he praises me. "Say my name."

Lick.

Suck.

Plunge of fingers.

"Beck," I moan, crazed with lust and adoration for this man worshipping between my legs. "Please."

"What do you want, Sela?"

"I want to come," I plead with him.

He pulls his mouth from me for a moment and it causes me to raise my head to look down at him. He gives me a mischievous grin. "Want to come by my mouth or cock?"

I give him a salacious smile back. "Both."

His teeth flash at me and he growls in appreciation. "Good fucking answer."

Beck then hits my clit hard, pursing his lips around it and sucking while he thrusts two fingers in and out of me. My pulse skyrockets, my hips gyrate in crazy circles attempting for more friction, and then he beats his tongue against me so hard and fast I splinter into a million fragments as my thighs tighten against his head while every muscle in my body trembles in release.

"O-o-o-o-h," I moan as the climax tears through me. "So good, Beck. So, so good."

I'm still trembling when Beck surges up my body, bringing my legs up high as they stay resting on his shoulders. My abdomen contracts inward as he folds me practically in half and then he's driving into me, bottoming out in one hard thrust.

"Goddamn," he grits out as he places both hands on the mattress for leverage. His eyes are glazed with lust but he manages to ask, "You okay?"

I nod, not really able to form coherent words of assent.

"Good, because I am going to fuck you so hard, Sela," he promises darkly as he starts pounding inside of me. "Going to come so deep in that pussy. Mark you as mine. It's my fucking pussy, you got that, baby? Mine."

His words thrill me. Dark, dirty, filthy words that speak to something deep inside of me. Knowing how turned on he is, how possessive of something that should only belong to me but truly doesn't. It's his to do with what he wants and he knows it.

It's purely ironic that after my rape, I always felt dirty . . . unworthy. It's why the barrier of a condom was more than a protection against pregnancy. It was a way for me to keep the dirt to myself and not taint another unsuspecting soul. While technically and from a purely health perspective, I'm as clean as they come, I always felt nasty when it comes to sex.

But not with Beck.

Not ever with Beck.

With every punch of his hips and every time his balls slap against my bottom, I feel whole and beautiful and completely worthy of what he's giving and taking.

Even as he's fucking me in this moment almost mindless with animalistic need, racing toward release the same as me, he makes me feel pure.

That's something I'm never giving up.

"Are you close?" Beck asks.

"Huh?" I groan as he tunnels deep into me.

"Close, baby. Are you close?"

"I think I am," I pant out as he continues to fuck me almost mercilessly.

"Need to know," he grunts. "Because I am and if you're not, I'm going to pull out and eat your pussy again."

Just the thought that he's so intent on getting me off again sparks that little kernel of tightly wound passion to start to expand and pulse deep within me. "Oh, I'm close all right," I tell him with an almost hysterical laugh.

"Good," he says, and doubles up on the pace of his fucking.

Beck's jaw tightens, his eyes focus on me with laserlike intensity, and he undulates against me in a perfect rhythm that seems to stroke every single inch of my flesh. His hips pump furiously and his cock hits me like a jackhammer, and he lets out a huge huff of breath just before his eyes squeeze shut.

It's almost in slow motion as I watch his brow furrow, his teeth grab on to his lower lip, and his head tilt back as he starts to come. It knocks and rattles my own orgasm loose and I cry out in surprise at its power.

Beck grinds into me and mutters, "Fuck. Fuck that's good. Fuck, Sela . . . coming inside of you is so goddamn good."

"Yes," I manage to gasp out as my channel clenches on to him tightly, ripples of pleasure going up and down my spine, curling my toes and my fingers almost spastically.

"Oh, Christ," Beck pants as he lowers my legs off his shoulders. I realize at once that I was barely able to breathe being almost folded in half, and a rush of oxygen into my lungs makes me dizzy.

It causes me to let out an almost maniacal laugh of relief as I suck in more air.

Beck drops down on top of me, holding most of his weight off by digging his elbows into the mattress. He presses his face into my neck, kisses me softly, and then pulls up to stare down at me.

"That was kind of 'wow,'" he says with a grin.

I nod, feeling lighter in heart and soul. Still that little bit of underlying sadness that my quest for vengeance is over, but considering what I just had with Beck . . . and that I could have that forever if I give this an honest effort, helps to lighten the burden of my loss somewhat.

Beck winds his hands under my back, rolls off me, and turns me into his arms until we are both lying on our sides face to face. He pushes a leg in between mine, brings a hand to the back of my head, and tucks it into the crook of his neck.

"When do you want to go to your dad's to get the decorations?" he asks while the fingers on his other hand stroke up the middle of my spine.

"This weekend?" I ask him back, assuming he can't take off time during the week. "I'm assuming he and Maria will want us to stay for dinner."

"How about Friday night?" he asks hesitantly.

"Sure. That will work."

We're silent for a moment and I start to relax into Beck's embrace, feeling sated and drowsy. I wonder what it would be like to take an afternoon nap with Beck. Just be naked and lazy in his arms.

"Sela?" Beck says after a cough that clears his throat. His voice is tense and hesitant.

"Yeah?"

"JT wants to get together with you and me for dinner on Saturday. I kind of accepted, but I totally understand if you don't want to go. I can make up an excuse or something."

There's no stopping the white-hot flash of rage that turns my blood to lava, and for an instant, I can't even speak because the feeling is so painful it robs me of words.

"I know you don't like him," Beck rushes onward. "He hasn't given you any room to, so I'm totally cool if you say no. It's just . . . he's still my business partner, and assuming he gets his shit together, I'm going to have to do functions with him and I hope you're by my side at them. You're going to run into him, and I thought . . . well, maybe you could get to know a little of the JT that I happen to like when he's on his A-game."

I take a deep breath in, let it out. Another in, let it out. I try to think calming thoughts and banish the red haze of fury from my vision.

"You're awful quiet," he says softly. "I'm taking this is going to be a no to the invitation."

I think about the red tattoo on Beck's back . . . a permanent part of him that I've decided to live with. I think of JT, the living embodiment of what that tattoo represents to me, and my choice to just live with what he's done. Can I seriously be around the man who brutalized me? Can I look him in the eye and have a polite conversation?

Will I ever be able to be in the same room with him and not lust with murder?

I don't know. It's unfathomable to me.

But I do know one thing.

I'm committing myself to Beck, and that means I've got to accept JT is in his life until such time as he screws up that privilege. Knowing JT, that will happen. A zebra doesn't change his stripes, I remind myself, and while he might be putting on a superlative effort to snow Beck at this moment, I know it's only a matter of time before he falls back onto his old, treacherous ways.

So I swallow my pride and my anger and my thirst for justice once again.

I do this all for Beck.

I commit myself even further to him when I say, "Sure. I might not like him very much, but I'll have dinner with him if that's what you want."

CHAPTER 22

Beck

"I'm a little ashamed," I say casually as we cruise through Sela's neighborhood. We hadn't talked much since heading out of San Francisco about forty-five minutes ago, the rush hour being hair-raising enough to require my full attention while Sela dug her nails into the supple leather of the passenger seat.

"Ashamed of what?" she asks, turning her head against the seat rest to look at me.

I spare just a moment to glance at her, but what a moment it is. Her hair is loose and flowing over her shoulders, and I ache to reach out to touch it because I know how soft it is. One of my favorite things now is Sela falling asleep on top of me and her hair resting like a silk blanket on my chest.

"That I didn't even know that you're from Belle Haven . . . practically my old stomping grounds," I tell her with a laugh as I put my eyes back on the road.

"Well, not really your old stomping grounds," she corrects me primly. "Belle Haven isn't exactly the hotbed of lifestyles of the rich and famous."

"Smartass," I grumble. "I just meant that you were minutes from me when I went to Stanford. We could have passed each other on the street at some point or even been at the same party together and never known it. Did you ever go to a lot of parties at Stanford?"

"No," she says softly as she gazes out the windows. "I wasn't much of a party girl."

The neighborhood of Belle Haven, located in Menlo Park, is no more than a couple of miles from Stanford in Palo Alto. It's a neighborhood that's had a very bad rap for years and years, and Sela's right . . . my family wouldn't be caught dead here once upon a time. But it's gotten better over the last five or so years, particularly with Facebook opening a campus here and pumping money into community programs. The violent crime rate has dropped drastically, which made it a good choice now for lower-income families.

Still, it's a far cry from where I grew up. My parents would be absolutely horrified to know I was involved with a woman from—gasp—the wrong side of the tracks. Imagining the looks on their faces actually gives me a warm, tingly feeling inside.

"It's that one right there," Sela says as she points to a tiny bungalow done in a light gray siding with a flat roof and a yellow porch light burning brightly. Even though it's already dark, there's plenty of light from the streetlamp, so I can see the lot is the size of a postage stamp with only ten feet or so in on either side of the house. Still, the yard is tidy with pretty bushes around the foundation and the drought-brown grass neatly edged at the sidewalk that runs adjacent to the road.

I park parallel on the street, as the short driveway has a white work truck and a small black car behind hit. Turning off the ignition, I say, "The family homestead. It's nice."

"Not a palace like you're used to," she says with a quirk to her lips.

Such beautiful lips.

So I lean over and give her a kiss. "I may have grown up in a monstrosity of a house, but it wasn't ever a home. Our condo . . . that's more of a home to me than I've ever lived in, and part of that is because you're there."

Sela's eyes fill with tenderness, a new look I'm liking on her face. The cool, aloof woman is warming up in ways I never imagined.

She reaches out, grabs my hand resting casually between us, and squeezes it. "You're too sweet to me."

"You make it easy," I assure her, actually enjoying the fact that these words of affection come easy to me.

Maybe I was built for relationships but just never found the right one. While Sela always maintains something in reserve that is still unknown to me, I've seen enough glimpses inside to know she could possibly be "the one." She's definitely worth the effort, and I hope that she'll fully open up to me one day. I've no doubt that something in her past keeps a part of her locked up tight from me, and that was evidenced by last week when she lied to me. Even thinking about it now, my shoulders tense up. I wasn't kidding with Sela . . . I don't abide by liars. I hate dishonesty and secrets and ulterior motives. I have reason to, and it's probably the only thing that could tear me away from her.

But ultimately, what Sela did was more of a fib than a lie. It was her terrible attempt to hide from me the fact she was feeling overwhelmed with everything that was occurring between us. Silly girl went for a walk to get her head on straight and didn't think I'd understand or be sympathetic to her doubts.

All of life is filled with doubt. All of us take calculated risks in our choices, and while I'm not one to second-guess myself, I fully understand that Sela might be having some difficulties in accepting what's going on between us. It's okay though . . . I'm a patient man.

I'm not going anywhere.

"Beck?" Sela asks softly.

"Yeah?"

"You're the first man I've brought home to meet my father."

I'm not surprised by this, but I am deeply flattered. Still, I know this is a big deal for her, but she's far too serious in this moment. I don't want this to be stressful on her, so I joke, "I won't embarrass you, I promise."

"You couldn't," she assures me, the joke bouncing off her shadowed eyes. "I'm not even quite sure why you're with someone like me."

I tilt my head, squeeze her hand, and admonish her, "If this is a shameless attempt to get me to extol all your virtues, we're going to be very late to dinner for me to take the time to do that."

She laughs softly, places her other hand over the ones we already have clasped. "No, it's just . . . sometimes on its face it's hard to see us together, you know? Different backgrounds, life choices, paths. I mean . . . think about it. You are so out of my league, Beck. If we hadn't met at that Sugar Bowl Mixer, chances are you and I would have never had the opportunity to even cross paths."

"And I certainly wasn't looking for a Sugar Baby," I tell her with a chuckle. "And I'm the one out of your league."

"But I *was* looking for a Sugar Daddy," she reminds me primly, refusing to debate league status.

"You got way more than you bargained for." I lower my voice

so it sounds ominous, "I've enjoyed corrupting you, Miss Halstead."

She snorts and releases my hands, grabs for the door handle. "I suggest you don't go saying shit like that around my father. He has guns in the house and he's just itching to play the role of overprotective father."

Laughing, I get out of the car and follow her up the sidewalk.

William Halstead is a good man. I figured it out from the minute he met us at the door and pulled Sela into a bear hug, rocking her back and forth and cooing, "There's my baby girl."

It was confirmed when he finally released her and gave me a hearty handshake, clasping my hand with two of his and pumping it vigorously while smiling at me as if I was a knight in shining armor. Sela wasn't kidding . . . I'm the first man she's ever brought home, and this apparently made her father very, very happy. It again makes me wonder how this smart, beautiful creature went so long without any real relationship. With regard to me, it's a no-brainer. My parents were terrible role models for what a healthy, loyal relationship should look like. But you can just tell that Sela grew up in a household with a lot of love and respect.

Perhaps, maybe like me, she was just waiting for the right one to come along.

I'm relieved that the conversation flowed easily throughout dinner. Sela's dad is a gregarious man and a natural-born storyteller. His girlfriend, Maria, is more reserved, but that could simply be because William tends to dominate conversations. I wonder if Sela's mom was that way as well.

"Can I get anyone anything to drink?" Maria asks as she walks into the living room. She had insisted on doing the dishes so we could all retire in here to talk and hang out for a bit before we headed back to the city.

"I'm good," I say, and Sela chimes in with, "I'm good too."

"I'm good, honey," William says as he reaches out to touch his hand to Maria's with a soft smile before she plops down onto the couch next to him.

Sela's body tightens next to me, barely perceptible, but I'm very in tune with her mood since we got here. While she is open and friendly with her father, she's a bit more reserved around Maria, and I know that has everything to do with the fact Sela fears this woman is replacing her late mother in her father's affections. She's not said much about it, but I can tell in the careful mask she keeps in place whenever she interacts with Maria.

"So tell me more about your business," William asks me, his hands folded casually over his stomach. William Halstead is a big man, in height and girth. Sela told me he heads the janitorial staff for the local high school and has been working there for nearly thirty years now. I do believe he's the first janitor I've ever known in my life, a thought that actually humbles me a bit.

"It's primarily a Web-based dating site that focuses on pairing wealthy men with women," I say, holding his gaze steady. Didn't think it would be this hard to tell Sela's dad what I did for a living, but I brace for censure.

"And it's called The Sugar Bowl?" Maria asks with a polite smile on her face. "What's that mean?"

Sela coughs slightly, and as she sits next to me on the love seat, I can see her from my peripheral vision put a hand over her mouth to hide a smirk. I think she's enjoying my discomfort a bit.

"It's a play on the words *sugar daddy,*" William says with booming voice. "I read an article online about it."

"What's a sugar daddy?" Maria asks, turning to look at William.

Sela nearly chokes and her dad shoots her a sly wink. He also saves me from having to explain by telling Maria, "Sugar daddy is a term used for a man who pays for everything for his woman."

Maria turns her brown eyes my way. She's an attractive Hispanic woman who made an amazing carne adobada for dinner and seemed to dote on Sela's dad. You can tell she's seriously in love with the man, but I could also tell that William holds something in reserve, sort of the way that Sela does with me. I wonder if Sela notices that and it makes her feel any better about him being with her.

"So, it's like Match.com, but it focuses more on economic factors?" she asks me, turning my way.

I nod and smile. "That's a good way to think of it."

Maria snorts and says, "Well, I can just imagine what those women have to do to land them a rich Sugar Daddy."

Sela chokes again, a snicker pops out, and she then lunges up off the couch, mumbling, "Excuse me. I need to use the restroom."

All three of us watch her walk away, and yeah . . . my eyes flip down to her retreating ass for a moment. Luckily, when I turn back to face William and Maria, they're still looking at the hallway where Sela just disappeared.

William slowly turns his face to me and says, "Well, it all sounds very impressive. I saw the net worth of your company."

And that embarrasses me a bit, making me feel slightly uncomfortable. I don't want Sela's dad to judge me on the merits of my bank account.

"She's an amazing girl," William says thoughtfully of his daughter. Maria reaches over and takes his hand, giving it a tiny pat of agreement. "She deserves nothing but the best."

"Agreed," I say.

"But she's also set in her ways," he continues, and this piques my interest. "She views this world in a certain way and sometimes has a hard time believing in the good of it. Be patient with her. Sela has a lot to offer anyone who has the pleasure of knowing her, but she can sometimes withdraw into herself. You ever catch her doing that, you pull her right back out again, okay?"

A sense of foreboding hits me, and a tiny spark of fear pulses within. William's words are so serious and at odds with the jovial dad of just a few minutes ago that was thrilled to have his daughter involved with a man for the first time in her life.

"I'm pretty sure there isn't anything I wouldn't do for Sela," I tell William solemnly, because I feel that he wants that type of promise. "I'll take care of her."

"Like a sugar daddy?" Maria asks, blinking innocent eyes at me.

I stare back at her completely stunned, my mouth hanging open. Then she starts laughing and points a finger at me while patting William on the leg. "You two need to lighten up. Sela's a strong girl and doesn't need a man making things right for her."

I suppose that's true, but as I look across the living room to William, I don't see him laughing along with Maria. Instead he pins me with a direct stare, conveying silently to me that he expects me to do exactly what I just promised him. And the look on his face says that if I don't, I will see a different side to Sela's dad.

CHAPTER 23

Sela

I slip on the Tag Heuer that Beck surprised me with last weekend when we spent a day shopping around San Francisco. After Caroline and Ally left, the apartment was almost stifling in its stillness, and he suggested a day out and about. It included a stop at an upscale jeweler where he insisted on buying me this stainless-steel beauty with a white ceramic face and diamonds around the edge, as well as twelve on the face for each hour. It's beautiful and so me; not too delicate, a little bold, and not the slightest bit ostentatious despite the high price tag. I put up an argument against his getting it for me, but Beck shut me up with a simple statement.

"Don't take this away from me. I've never had anyone I could buy jewelry for."

Checking the time, I note I have about ten minutes before I have to get down to the lobby so the doorman can hail me a cab. Tonight's the big dinner with JT and my nerves have been vibrating all day. Beck got called into the office about three hours ago, something I didn't quite understand. He's the freakin' owner of a multimillion-dollar business and yet he was spending his Saturday at the office helping programmers with some meddlesome code. Beck explained to me that they were launching a new platform at the beginning of the year, and while that was still thirty days away, the work was round the clock to meet the deadline. When the programmers got stuck, Beck was the big cheese, and this was his baby, so he went in to work. He took a suit with him, since we were dining in a very fancy and posh restaurant, and gave me a long, sizzling kiss to help ease the sting of ditching me today.

I easily forgave him though. It was hard not to after the wonderful time we had with my dad last night, who very much liked and approved of Beck. Before we left, he gave me an all-encompassing hug and whispered in my ear, "I'm really happy for you, honey."

I'm happy for me too.

Will be much happier if I can get past tonight.

There is no doubt in my mind that I'm getting ready to face an incredibly hard few hours. To sit at a table with my rapist—a man who is so vile I want to scratch his eyes out and castrate him at the same time—has me wondering if I have the mettle within me to pull off such an act.

I should be able to do it. The first few weeks with Beck, much of what I showed him was nothing but a superb performance worthy of an Oscar. But that façade soon gave way to feelings and emotions that were genuine to my soul, and as I stand here now, looking in the mirror above the sink vanity, I know that if I'm going to keep the purity of my relationship with Beck, I need to stick to my new quest. I need to release my need for vengeance and pour my efforts into a relationship with a man I've come to care deeply for. In my heart, I know that my rewards will be infinitely greater if I manage to pull this off.

The doorbell rings and it startles me. No one ever comes to Beck's condo unless it's for a delivery of some sort, and I've found out that Beck likes to have things delivered to me. I've received countless flowers, candy, and even a set of naughty lingerie that he received the benefit of that one night when I greeted him at the door wearing it.

In fact, I'm betting there's probably a bouquet of daisies and freesia waiting on the other side, probably an unnecessary apology from Beck for his bailing on me today.

Smiling, I walk down the hallway, past the large dining room table and into the foyer, my heels clacking on the hardwood flooring. I pull the door open, expecting the smell of flowers to hit me, and instead find myself facing Jonathon Townsend.

He stands there casually, both hands tucked into the pockets of an expensive pair of black dress pants. His suit jacket is unbuttoned, showcasing a pristine starched white shirt underneath, sans tie and unbuttoned at his throat.

His eyes pin me in place and he gives me a smile that falls somewhere between licentious and bland. "Hello, Sela."

My fingers tighten on the knob and I resist the urge to slam the door in his face. I swallow past the dryness in my throat, will my heart rate to calm down, and ask, "What are you doing here?"

"Knew Beck was at work. He said you were taking a cab to the restaurant, so I had my driver stop by and figured I'd offer you a ride. We still have to swing by and pick up my date, of course, but she's just a few blocks down."

The room spins a little at the prospect of sitting in a car with this man, but I can't think of a sane reason to decline his invitation. It would be utterly ludicrous for me to insist I take a cab, and the only thing it would serve would be the fact it would make a very clear statement that I detest him. While I'm not in the slightest bit worried about hurting his feelings, I also don't want to make this evening any more unpleasant than I already know it will be. If I antagonize him now, I know the type of person JT is. He'll make it rough on all of us tonight.

And besides . . . I promised myself I'd never, ever do anything to let him know that I fear him. Because I don't. I detest and hate him. Loathe him so much that periodic flashes of murder will still pop within my mind. I know Jonathon is the type of man who likes to intimidate women. It makes him feel better about himself, so I'll be damned if I'm ever going to help him do that.

So I take a deep breath and decide the sooner I get this evening started, the sooner it will be over, and I can do this for Beck.

"Let me grab my purse," I say, my voice sounding frosty and not the least bit grateful, so I make a concerted effort. "Thank you for thinking of me."

I turn to the foyer table, pick up the black clutch I bought this weekend with some of my own money. It matches the black cocktail dress I have on, also bought with my money. I turn to JT and find his gaze lowered, clearly having been staring at my ass as I turned around. At this moment I wish my gun were in my purse, so I could pull it out and shoot him in the balls before putting a bullet in his brain.

His gaze comes up my body lazily and he gives me a sheepish smile. "Sorry."

Not sounding the least bit apologetic.

I don't respond but brush past him, pulling the door shut behind me.

I'm silent as we make our way down to the lobby and I'm relieved when I see a driver standing next to an open door of a limousine with his hand extended to help me in. I'd hate for JT to get an attack of gentlemanly airs and try to give me assistance. As it is, I can feel his eyes on my ass again as I get in, which ensures the simmering anger continues to froth and bubble within my stomach. I wish I'd thought to put a pack of Tums in my purse.

JT thankfully takes the seat opposite of me and we pull away from the curb. He sits with his legs spread slightly and his hands resting on his thighs. He looks at me appraisingly, and says, "I don't think you'll like my date, or have much in common with her."

I blink in surprise, his voice sounding aloof and with airs typical of someone of his breeding. I cock at eyebrow. "Oh, why's that?"

I'm not imagining the slight curl to his lip, and while his voice is mild and pleasant enough, his snub is clear from his words. "It's just she's from money. Very old San Francisco money. Has the requisite blue in her blood, a fancy degree from Brown, and probably saving her virginity for marriage. You two would have nothing in common."

And in this moment, it's clear to me that not only is JT a rapist, a vile human being, and an abuser of women and his friends, but that he clearly doesn't like me at all. In fact, I'd even say there's a level of jealousy within his voice that speaks to his concern that I might turn his close friend and business partner against him.

This flushes me with power and I just smile at him sweetly. "It's true . . . I lost my virginity a long time ago." *To you, you fucking slime-sucking piece of shit.* "But Beck certainly likes what he sees in me."

"I'm sure," he says with a polite smile on his face, but his words are dry as the desert earth.

The limo comes to a slow halt in front of an expensive condominium and I can hear the driver get out. JT just stares at me across the expanse of the interior, and I turn my head to look out the window at the entrance doors.

"Aren't you going to go up and get her?" I ask as I swivel my head back to look at him.

"I had the driver call her when we left your place," he says with a wave of his hand. "Besides . . . I don't want Amelia thinking this is anything more than an arranged dinner between our meddling mothers. She's got marriage stars in her eyes and I don't want them getting any brighter."

What an asshole.

The door opens and I see a petite blond woman walking toward the car, a beige clutch in her perfectly manicured hand. She's got on a beige skirt and matching suit jacket with big black buttons that run up the side, and a pair of black heels that I'm betting cost more than my entire wardrobe. Her hair is done in a perfect chignon and her makeup is flawless. Large diamonds wink in her ears that I'm betting are no smaller than four carats.

The driver helps her into the car as JT slides over, and she sits down beside him, shooting me a quick glance.

She leans over and offers her cheek to JT. I'm wrapped up in a cloud of her perfume as I watch him kiss her cheek before turning to me.

"Amelia . . . this is Beck's date tonight, Sela Halstead. Sela, this is Amelia Baxter."

I smile and extend my hand across the limo. "Hello. Nice to meet you."

She offers a return smile that's neither warm nor cold, but merely accommodating, and shakes my hand. "It's lovely to meet you."

Amelia then turns from me and bestows a gorgeous smile on

JT. "And how have you been doing, Jonathon? I can't tell you how excited I was to get your call inviting me out tonight. I know our mothers have been trying to throw us together for years, so I hope this wasn't their doing and that you've finally come to your senses."

She gives a tinkling giggle and slaps her hand playfully on his chest. She stares at him with bright, earnest eyes, hoping beyond hope that she may have caught more than just a dinner date tonight. I can practically see her fantasizing about the size of the engagement ring she'll put on her finger, and it makes me feel incredibly sad for her.

JT shrugs carelessly and turns his gaze to me while answering her question. "It's just dinner, Amelia. So I can spend time getting to know Beck's new Sugar Baby."

While I can tell Amelia is immediately stung by his snub, she turns her head to me with eyes wide. She takes a cursory glance at my outfit, and then wrinkles her nose in distaste before turning back to JT. "She's a Sugar Baby?"

Before JT can answer, I tell her. "JT's mistaken. I'm not a Sugar Baby. I'm Beck's girlfriend."

"But Beck paid for your college, right?" JT says, and it irks me that he knows that. Irks me a little that Beck told him that, which makes me feel less than what I'd believed I was to him.

"Yes, but we did away with our agreement," I say, my voice slightly shaking in anger and embarrassment.

JT shrugs again and turns to Amelia. His hand drops to her thigh, which is more than adequately covered by her sedate skirt that doesn't even have a slit in it. His gaze roams over her face and his hand slides higher up her leg. He leans over, whispering in her ear still plenty loud enough for me to hear. "You look beautiful tonight. New blond highlights?"

His hand slides up a little higher and Amelia's face goes red.

Not sure if it's from his creeping hand or the compliment he just paid her hair, which seriously . . . what guy ever notices shit like that?

Amelia nervously pats the back of her chignon and nods. "I did in fact get new highlights. I'm glad you like them."

JT's long fingers grip into her thigh, his hand resting practically near her hip. He growls seductively at her and murmurs, "Well, you know I love blondes."

My lips curl in absolute disgust. I can tell that JT doesn't have an ounce of attraction toward Amelia other than perhaps wanting to fuck her tonight because she's handy and available. I imagine it will be quick and focused only on getting his rocks off, and I'm sure he'll leave her the minute he pulls out. Watching Amelia blush again and then give a little sigh of appreciation makes me even more sad for her.

I start to turn my head to look out the window, but JT's gaze snaps back over to mine, halting me. He stares at me a moment and then his lips curve upward. "You know, Sela . . . I think you'd make a terrific-looking blonde."

My gut churns, and is it my imagination, or is that a taunt?

"I mean . . . you're stunning as a brunette, but I think blond would look more natural with your skin tone. Of course, I can't say what Beck's preference is. He's an equal opportunity man . . . fucked blondes, brunettes, redheads. He loves them all."

His direct attempt to make me jealous is almost pathetic because he rattled me enough with the blonde comment and it wasn't needed. I can't tell to what extent JT is fucking with me, and I'm wondering if he knows who I am. I can't imagine it. He's too self-centered to recognize the woman he destroyed all those years ago. I'm sure of it.

Amelia makes a sound of dismay deep in her throat, because she's not missed the seductive nature of JT's tone when he told me I would look natural as a blonde. She sniffs and says, "Honestly, JT. That's crude to say right in front of your date."

"It's not a date, Amelia," he says, his eyes still trained on me. "It's a favor owed to my mother. Don't make it more than what it is."

I wince, because that was harsh.

Amelia gasps and her face flames red. "Well, I don't think this night is exactly what I had anticipated, so if you don't mind, I'd like for you to just take me back—"

JT spins on her and his hand flexes, digging down into her thigh. Amelia's mouth snaps shut in surprise and she even leans back a little from JT when he presses toward her. His voice is soft, low, and rich with promise as he plays her right into his hands. "But relax, Amelia. I'm sure it has the potential to be so much more."

And just like that, she melts into him. I see the fantasy of the engagement ring getting bigger as her hand covers his on her thigh and she sighs like a lovestruck puppy. Just like that, JT managed to insult her and then have her practically spreading her virgin legs for him.

It sickens me, and the bubbling in my gut burns hotter.

Thankfully, I'm spared any more of JT's mind fucks as the limo pulls up in front of the restaurant. JT turns to me, nods with a condescending smirk, and I curl my fingers into my hands to stop my own fantasy made real of clawing his eyes out.

Then the door is opening and I see Beck standing there beside the driver, his eyes warm upon me. He extends his hand and I take it, letting him help me from the car, where he pulls me right into an embrace.

"Hey," he says, snuggling his face into my neck before pulling back and giving me a soft kiss on my lips. "You look fantastic."

"Thanks," I murmur as he pulls me back a few steps so JT and Amelia can get out of the car. "You look amazing too."

And he does, the dark gray of his suit setting off those light blue eyes as they stare at me with happiness.

"You okay?" Beck asks as he looks down at me.

"Sure," I say with a smile, trying to relax my facial features that still may have been holding some disgust over JT's behavior in the car. "Just happy to see you."

Beck likes that . . . I can tell because he gives me another kiss as his hand squeezes my waist reflexively. Then he releases me, turns to Amelia, and bends over to kiss her cheek. "Amelia . . . good to see you."

I'm not surprised Beck knows her. I knew JT's and Beck's mothers ran in the same social circles, so I figured they were all just one big, happy clique of rich friends.

Then Beck reaches his hand out toward JT. "Thanks for picking my girl up."

JT takes Beck's hand and gives him a warm grin before pulling him in and giving him a half hug while they clap each other on the back. "What are friends for?" JT says as he squeezes Beck in a brotherly embrace.

My eyes trail up to Beck's face, and I almost reel back from what I see.

Beck beaming pure happiness to be here with his buddy.

Grateful his friend looked out for his girl for him.

Beck completely stoked with the new "JT" and completely oblivious to the fact his friend and business partner is a douche and a rapist.

Willing to let him back into his life as if there's nothing to worry about and all of the shitty things JT's done are simply forgiven and forgotten.

The burning in my stomach turns hotter.

CHAPTER 24

Beck

"Good morning," Linda chirps as I walk by her desk.

"Morning," I grumble, completely not feeling her sunny attitude.

She stands up from her chair, grabs some folders off her desk, and follows me into my office. "Well, you're all bright and chipper this morning," she says sarcastically.

"And not in the mood," I tell her darkly as I plop down in my chair before rolling my mouse across the pad to disengage my screensavers.

Her voice is brisk and efficient when she lays the folders on my desk. "Mr. Townsend would like you to go over these proposals, and your two o'clock meeting got pushed back to three because Mr. Perkins' flight got delayed out of LaGuardia."

I reach for the folders and flip through them briefly with a sigh. "Okay, thank you, Linda."

"Anything else you need from me right now?"

"No, I'm good," I tell her distractedly as I log on to the system. She turns to leave and then I change my mind. "Wait . . . I could use some help locating a service that could deliver a Christmas tree to the condo."

Linda just blinks at me, confusion reigning supreme on her face. "I'm sorry?"

"A tree . . . you know, something green and Christmasy-smelling that Sela and I can decorate."

A bright, knowing smile spreads across Linda's face, making the wrinkles at her eyes and corners of her mouth deepen with romantic appreciation. "Oh, that's lovely. Of course I can locate something. Would you like something in spruce, or maybe pine? Those smell so good."

Shaking my head, I give her a quick eye roll and tell her, "I don't care. Just see if you can get something delivered today. Sela will be there all day."

Lying in bed moping, I'm sure, but she'll be there all day.

Linda leaves and closes the door behind her. Rather than jump into work, I turn my chair to look out the windows, contemplating the conundrum that Sela has recently become. While our dinner with her dad and Maria went fantastically Friday night, things started going downhill on Saturday. I don't think she was mad that I couldn't pick her up, but she was almost coldly reserved during dinner with JT and Amelia.

And I didn't get it.

JT was making an honest effort with Sela. From the moment we all sat down at the restaurant, he was charming and tried to engage her. He spoke warmly to her, was interested in her background, and tried to win her over with absolutely no success. I know he may have been laying it on a little thick, but JT was trying. He was happy that I found someone, and he could guess well enough that Sela was in my life to stay and he was honestly trying. He'd shown up at work every day fresh and lucid, rolling up his shirtsleeves and diving back into his business with renewed vigor and passion. We joked around like the old days, and it was even refreshing to see him with Amelia. She's a sweet girl, a little naïve, but JT doted on her all night. When it became clear that Sela wasn't going to participate in the conversation with JT, he turned his polite and engaging attention on Amelia, making her preen and swoon under his attention. It was the JT of old . . . the one who made me excited with the possibilities of a bright future.

It was the JT I recognize on a cellular level.

That night, Sela and I cabbed it home, but she maintained her aloofness with me, claiming she wasn't feeling well when we climbed into bed. I thought this might be a brush-off, but she had no hesitation in letting me at least pull her into my arms to go to sleep. It was the first night we hadn't had sex since we'd been together, and I wasn't put off by that. I was more worried about her cold attitude toward JT, but maybe she just needed more time to warm up to him. I'm sure he could win her over eventually if he kept on this path.

I figured Sunday would dawn bright, and I'd have the old Sela back. I found her up and in the kitchen when I awoke, sipping coffee and surfing the Internet on her laptop she'd bought last week. Winter semester had started, and when I walked in to kiss her on the top of her head, I saw she was reading an article entitled "Psychology of Criminal Behavior."

"Class you're taking?" I asked.

"Yeah," she said distractedly, leaning in closer as her eyes raced across the screen.

"Cool," I said as I moved over to pour myself some coffee. She ignored me, the fingers of one hand idly circling the top of her mug that I know held tea. She religiously had two cups every morning.

"Want to put up the decorations today?" I asked, figuring that would get her attention.

I was surprised when she shook her head, "No. I've got a few chapters to read before Tuesday's classes, so I thought I'd get a head start on that."

Staring at the back of her head, I tried to figure out what the fuck was going on with her. Just two days ago she was practically jumping with excitement as we drove back to San Francisco, the backseat and trunk of the Audi loaded with boxes of lights, ornaments, a ceramic Christmas village her mom hand-painted, and a collection of what I considered to be hideous nutcracker Santas.

Something was fucking wrong, and I'm not one to beat around the bush. "What's going on, Sela?"

She kept her back turned to me, face closer to the laptop. "Nothing," she said in a voice that clearly said she didn't even take note of the worry in my tone.

I walked up to the table, reached out, and put my hand in front of the screen to break her concentration. She looked up at me with those blue eyes and blinked in surprise.

So I repeated, "What's wrong?"

"There's nothing wrong," she said calmly. "I just don't feel like decorating today."

"Try again," I said as I gently closed the laptop and pulled the adjacent chair out. I sat down, took her hands in mine, and squeezed them. "You clearly didn't enjoy last night. You barely said two words at dinner even though I thought JT did an admirable job trying to include you in the discussion. And now you don't want to decorate for Christmas when you were about ready to pee your pants just a few days ago over the prospect, so I repeat . . . what's wrong?"

I thought the fact I called her out on her behavior at dinner would cause her to turn sheepish and apologetic; maybe get an admission that she's being a bit unfair to JT, but instead her eyes flashed with both fire and ice at the same time. It was such a powerful array of emotions that I flinched.

Her voice was frigid when she said, "I'm sorry if I embarrassed you last night, but clearly I just didn't enjoy the company. So fucking sue me."

Every instinct in my body wanted to rail against her outright refusal to cut JT a break, but I took a deep breath and tried to remain calm. "Sela . . . he tried last night. Why couldn't you?"

"It doesn't matter," she said in a quiet voice, and tried to pull her hands away from mine.

"It does matter," I said softly, holding on to her tight. "JT's my partner . . . my friend. Yeah, he's been a prick in the past, and maybe still will be in the future, but last night . . . he was trying hard for you."

"He was trying hard for *you*," she bit out.

"For both of us," I counter, and reach a hand up to her cheek. "He likes seeing me happy. He wanted last night to be fun for both of us. Hell, I think he's even taking a page from my book and maybe thinking of settling down. He and Amelia seemed pretty taken with each other last night."

Sela snorted, brought a hand to her mouth, and covered it so I wouldn't see the smirk on her lips. But I saw it in her eyes. "Last night was an act. He suckered you."

"That's a little harsh," I reprimanded her. "Where's the benefit of the doubt?"

"It got erased in the limo ride over," she snarled at me.

"Why? What happened?" My chest got tight and anger surged within me. It made it clear that while I thought JT did an admirable job last night, just those simple words from Sela had me thinking the worst about him again. Clearly, I didn't have the whole "benefit of the doubt" thing down to a science.

Sela leaned in toward me and said, "Nothing other than he was unbelievably rude to me and Amelia on the way to the restaurant. Made sure to point out all the ways I don't measure up for you."

"What did he say?" I asked, my voice forged with steel.

"Just pointed out all of Amelia's good breeding and pedigrees and told her I was a Sugar Baby," she spat out.

I smiled at her and tried for my most soothing voice. "Baby . . . he knew you started out as a Sugar Baby. I'm sure he was just trying to make conversation—"

Sela screeched at me and launched up from her chair. "Don't you dare fucking defend him. You weren't there . . . you don't know."

Her face was red and her eyes moist with frustration. I reached out to her but she spun away, ran down the hall to our bedroom. I followed her in there, finding her shoving her feet into her tennis shoes before grabbing a sweatshirt from the closet.

"What are you doing?"

"I'm going to the library to study on campus," she gritted out, brushing back past me. I followed her back into the kitchen where she shoved her laptop in her backpack and slung it over her shoulder.

"Sela, just stop for a minute," I said softly.

"I can't talk to you about this right now," she huffed, and barreled past me toward the door. I thought about grabbing her arm, making her stay, but anger started to flush through me over this bratty behavior. Clearly something must have happened to piss her off even more with JT, but she wasn't seeing reason.

And frankly, I didn't think forcing her to converse at this point would do any good in her current state of mind.

"I'll be gone all day," she muttered as she jerked the door open.

"Fine," I snapped back her. "Maybe you'll be in a more sane mood when you get back."

It was a shitty thing to say, and yet it felt good at the same time. Her bizarre behavior had left me reeling and I wasn't thinking clearly either.

She turned that beautiful face my way, looking at me over her shoulder. Her face was filled with anger and disappointment. She looked at me only a moment before she walked out and slammed the door behind her.

I spent the morning watching TV. I checked my watch about a thousand times. I made a sandwich for lunch and watched two football games. I made another sandwich for dinner, and still Sela hadn't returned.

I then decided to get some work done and locked myself away in my office. It was almost eight o'clock when I heard the condo door open and close.

Heard her tennis shoes squeaking on the floor as she walked down the hallway to our bedroom.

I considered following her, testing the waters to see where her head was at. But I didn't. I worked another two hours, and when I finally decided to go to bed, I found her sleeping on her side of the mattress, breathing deeply. I got undressed, brushed my teeth, and slid in to bed, wanting to pull her into my arms. I debated about it, wondering if it would wake her up. I even considered putting my hand between her legs and forcing her to give me something.

Instead, I just turned over on my side and watched my bedside clock tick away the time. It was well after midnight before I finally fell asleep.

When I woke up the next morning with my alarm buzzing at 6:30 A.M., I found Sela's body wrapped around me. We both lay in the center of the bed, somehow coming together in our sleep. I held her for a bit, relishing this warm woman who was quickly becoming my entire world, and wondering what I could do to fix things between us.

Apparently it didn't take much, because Sela stirred in my arms and burrowed her face into my neck.

"I'm sorry about yesterday," she said, her voice husky with sleep.

"Shh," I said in response, really not needing the apology. I just wanted things to be okay. I just wanted us talking again, and this was a damn good start.

Sela then surprised me by dropping her hand to my stomach, pushing downward until she found my soft cock. The minute her fingers grasped it, it started thickening and I arched my hips.

In the gloomy dawn hours, Sela straddled my hips, guided me inside her, and rode me to perfect completion. She was silent as she did so, her hands on my chest and her gaze solemn as she bounced up and down on my dick. The only way I knew it felt good to her was just moments before I came, her nails scored my chest and her head tipped back as she groaned out an unbelievably hard orgasm that left her shaking, and her pussy clamped down hard on me. I followed her immediately, punching my hips up and pulling her down for a long kiss.

I thought things might be okay. I got out of bed and showered. Her eyes followed me around the room as I got dressed, her cheeks flushed pink from that amazing fucking we just did and appreciation of my body. I loved her eyes on me so much.

Yeah . . . I thought it would be fine. Except when I went to kiss her goodbye, I asked her if she was interested in decorating the condo tonight when I got home. I thought that might get a renewed smile out of her. She merely shrugged her shoulders and said, "Maybe. Let's see how I feel."

And that made me realize things weren't good at all.

CHAPTER 25

Sela

It took no more than two minutes before I heard Beck leave the condo before I was up out of bed and getting my day started. I took a quick shower. I didn't bother with makeup but gave my teeth a good brushing before twisting and clipping my wet hair to the back of my head.

In ten minutes, I was dressed and had my first cup of tea. I even took the time to make toast with butter and jam and eat it.

Then I walked into our bathroom, grabbed my makeup bag, and pulled out the key to Beck's office.

I slid it in the lock and it turned as easily as cutting through butter with a warm knife. I opened the door and took stock of my feelings. Not an ounce of guilt possessed me.

Nothing but raw determination.

While I might have hesitated before in making this move, I did so back when my feelings for Beck were solid. But after Saturday night, when I saw just how easy Beck was letting JT back into his life, and with Beck just yesterday defending that lecherous bastard to me, I knew I couldn't let those feelings interfere anymore.

Yes, there are feelings. Deep, abiding, overwhelming feelings I have for Beck. But they are now tempered with bitter hatred that resurfaced toward JT Saturday night. It might not have been so bad just suffering JT's slights and innuendos. I probably could have handled that.

But I felt something grow cold inside of me when I watched Beck and JT hugging it out all bro style outside the restaurant. I saw renewed respect in Beck's eyes, and happiness to be in JT's presence. I watched all through dinner as they told war stories and shared memories of growing up together, and it filled me with such bitterness I had to choke down my meal.

While I loved Beck inside me this morning, I rode him with a slight hardening of my heart, instead focusing on just the bodily pleasures we could bestow on each other. I had Beck and I wasn't prepared to give him up, but I wasn't prepared to give up myself either.

And to be true to myself, I have accepted that I'm going to have to make JT suffer for what he did. I'm going to obliterate him from this earth, and not only will that avenge the atrocities he dealt me, it will free Beck from that monster as well. I consider this a mission of liberation for us both, and if there's something in this office that can help me, I'm going to utilize it.

Infiltrate.

Murder.

Repeat.

Very simple.

I look around and take in Beck's office. It's sparse and utilitarian, holding nothing but a desk with a computer and two monitors, as well as a four-drawer filing cabinet in the corner. I don't give the computer another glance, knowing that I'll never be able to break into it past Beck's password. He's too savvy to ever be that stupid.

Instead I walk around the desk, sit in the mesh Herman Miller chair and pull open the first drawer on the right. It contains hanging file folders and I pull them all out, roughly ten, stuffed full of papers. I open the top one and see bank statements with reconciliations stapled to the front. Flipping through, it looks like all of Beck's personal banking accounts. Two checking and three money markets. The balances within are hefty but that doesn't impress me. I know Beck's rich.

The next folder holds a thick document entitled "The Beckett W. North, Jr., Trust and Pour-Over Will." I scan it briefly and it essentially leaves everything to Caroline, including his ownership of Townsend-North Holdings, with it going to Ally if Caroline dies first. The next folder contains a separate trust for Ally that he set up and apparently contributes a percentage of his profits to monthly.

The next folder holds paperwork for a 529 plan for Ally. Her college is completely funded.

I set that aside and open the next folder, finding my original Sugar agreement that I signed with Beck along with receipts for the monies he paid me and to Golden Gate for my tuition. PAID IN FULL is scrawled in blue ink on the agreement

Looks like I'm a paid Sugar Baby after all, I think bitterly.

I set that folder aside and flip through the others. His lease agreement for the Audi; the closing documents for the condo he bought two years ago; another folder with a mutual fund portfolio. All stuff that's completely uninteresting to me and doesn't tell me a damn thing about Jonathon Townsend.

I complete my perusal, growing more frustrated by the second. Still, I take the time to carefully put them back in the drawer as best I can remember they were arranged.

My eyes then drift to the four-drawer filing cabinet.

I push out of the chair and walk up to it, opening the top drawer. I'm immediately rewarded with a folder labeled TOWNSEND-

NORTH HOLDINGS. I pull it out and remove a thick document entitled "Partnership Agreement." On the first page, I see introductory language regarding the formation of a partnership between Jonathon Townsend and Beckett North, with both of their home addresses following right behind.

Bingo.

I at least have one solid piece of information.

I know where JT lives now.

Don't think me a fool. I've tried desperately to find his home address, but that's some supersecret shit that the wealthy and famous alike can hide to protect their anonymity. I'm sure I could have found it before now with the help of a private investigator, but I didn't have the funds for that. This little tidbit saves me the trouble of following him home from work one night, which I was more than willing to do.

I scramble back to Beck's desk, open the top middle drawer, and find a square pad of yellow paper. I pull it out with a pen and scribble down the address before tucking it into my back pocket. I flip through the pages of the agreement and don't see anything that will help me further, so I tuck it back into the folder.

I then put my fingers on the next one behind it, but pause when I see the writing on the tab: SCHAEFER—CRIMINAL INVESTIGATION.

Confused beyond measure, I reach for the folder, intent on discovering what secrets Beck is hiding. My fingers grasp onto a thick sheaf of papers inside, and just as I pull them out, a shadow falls across me.

I turn my face slowly toward the door, and see Beck standing there, his eyes wide and condemning.

"What in the fuck are you doing?" he asks slowly through gritted teeth as he walks into the office, his face contorting with rage.

I'm so stunned to see him there I can't even force out an explanation. He stalks up to me, pulls the folder from my hand, and throws it sideways across the room, where it smacks against the wall of windows and the papers come loose, spilling to the floor.

"Beck," I manage to croak out, holding my arms out in front of me defensively.

His hand shoots out, grabs me above my elbow. He leans his face in and snarls, "You fucking broke into my office?"

He's furious, and tiny bits of spittle hit my cheek. I reach my free hand up to wipe it away but he's dragging me out of the office, so I just flail for balance.

"Jesus Christ," he snarls as he pulls me into the hallway. "Who the fuck are you? What's your goddamn game, Sela?"

"Beck," I implore as he manhandles me into the living room. "Just wait . . ."

"I fucking trusted you," he yells in his rampage, refusing to look at me. "I brought you into my home, into my bed . . . and you've been doing nothing but lying to me, sneaking behind my back. Are you a fucking spy for another company? What's the game, Sela?"

His fingers are digging into my arm so hard my bone aches. My free hand comes up and tries to peel his fingers back to give me respite. He's holding me so tightly, though, I can't make any headway. I dig down the heels of my tennis shoes and they catch on the hardwood floor, except Beck is pulling me so hard I go flying face forward and fall to my knees. Beck pauses . . . gives me a moment to stand up, and the minute I'm upright, he starts pulling me forward again.

"I want you out of my fucking condo," he snarls, and I see he's heading for the front door.

I redouble my efforts trying to dig my heels in again, but Beck doesn't even pause. He jerks on my arm, causing me to stumble, and reaches for the doorknob.

"Beck, no . . . wait," I plead with him. "Please give me a chance to explain."

"What's to explain?" he asks with a bitter laugh as he releases his hold and spins on me. "You know . . . that day you lied to me about taking my car. I knew something was up then. My gut told me there was something you were hiding."

"It's not what you think," I say as I shake my head in denial at him.

"Broke into my office, and looking for shit on me," he spits out at me with disgust.

"No . . . I swear to you," I say in a half sob, and finally blurt out, "It's about JT."

Beck throws his head back and gives a sarcastic, bitter bark of a laugh. His eyes shine with malice as he grabs my purse off the foyer table and shoves it right into my chest. My hands come up automatically to catch it as he releases, and I hug it to me. "Don't even go there, Sela. You've had a hard-on for him for some reason, but I've known him forever. I've known you for a few weeks. What you and I have can never compare to the bond I have with him. Who the fuck do you think I'm going to believe?"

"I swear to God, Beck . . . this is about JT," I say as tears now spring to my eyes, fill them to the brim, and with just one slight blink of my lids, go spilling over.

"Save it," he growls, and his hand shoots back out to latch on to my upper arm now. He gives me a hard jerk, and I go stumbling forward again. He grabs the doorknob, wrenches it open, and starts pushing me through. "I want you out of here now. I'll pack your shit up and have it delivered to your apartment, but you get the fuck out of my home and out of my life right this very minute and don't look backward."

"Beck," I wail, dropping my purse on the foyer floor as I reach out to him, desperately trying to get him to listen to me. "I swear I'm not trying to hurt you."

His blue eyes fill with darkness and his eyes narrow at me with something I would put akin to hatred. His hand shoots out and he catches me around the front of my neck, pulling me in slowly and up onto my tiptoes until he's almost nose to nose with me. For the first time since he caught me in his office, his tone is calm but still rippling with rage and menace. "You're no better than all the other girls, Sela. All looking to get ahead at some man's expense. What were you doing? Searching my financials? Hoping to blackmail me with something? Looking to steal from me?"

With each question he asks, his grip on my throat tightens but not enough to cut off my air. Only enough to keep my attention and so I don't forget he's in control of this situation right now. With each question, his fury seems to increase, as if my inability to answer is an admission to each accusation.

He pulls me in a fraction of an inch closer and whispers, "I don't care what the reason. I just want you fucking gone."

Beck pushes me through the door and I have no choice but to walk backward from the force of his grip on me. My hands fly out, grab on to each side of the doorjamb, and dig in hard.

"Let go, Sela," he snarls at me, releasing his hand on my throat and capturing both my wrists tightly with his hands. He peels them loose.

"No, wait," I cry out, trying to launch myself back into the doorway.

"Get the fuck out," he bellows at me with so much rage it feels like a sonic boom reverberating in my ears.

Beck pushes me hard, lets go of my wrists, and I stumble backward, falling to my butt with a jarring impact. He kicks at my purse, sending it hurtling through the door where the contents spill out all over the floor. That doesn't stop me though. I immediately lurch forward to my hands and knees, crawling toward Beck standing in the door.

"Please listen to me, Beck," I implore, my eyes begging him for just a few moments of his mercy.

He glares down at me, complete and utter disgust holding every inch of his beautiful face hostage. I crawl faster as he starts to shut the door, reaching one hand out in a pitiful attempt for a single, fucking bit of leniency from this man. He looks down at me like he wants to spit on me.

"Beck," I say with a sob.

The door is halfway closed and I take a desperate look at his face, knowing that it's the last time I'll ever see it again. I'll never know pleasure and joy like he's given me, and although I know I've betrayed him and I can't blame him for his actions right now, I throw all caution to the wind and I bare my soul to him. "JT . . . he raped me."

The door comes to an immediate halt and Beck's eyes go round with surprise. His mouth slackens and he pales for a moment as he looks down at me, his head tilted in confusion. I think perhaps he may even reach a hand out toward me . . . help me to my feet . . . pull me into his embrace and tell me it's all going to be okay.

I even go so far as to reach my hand upward to him.

Instead, his eyes go cold, his lips flatten out, and he shakes his head at me in disgust. "Yet another lie, Sela."

Then he slams the door in my face.

AUTHOR'S NOTE

I hope you enjoyed the sexy, thrilling ride of *Sugar Daddy*. This novel is different from anything I've written before. Find out what happens between Beck and Sela in *Sugar Rush* and the conclusion to their story, *Sugar Free,* both coming in 2016.

Read on for an excerpt from

Sugar Rush

by Sawyer Bennett
Available from Loveswept

CHAPTER 1

Sela

I throw all caution to the wind and I bare my soul to him. "JT . . . he raped me."

Cold eyes.

Look of disgust.

"Yet another lie, Sela."

Then he slams the door in my face.

Pain such as I've never felt seizes my chest.

It's like a blackened claw wrapping around my heart, squeezing so hard it robs me of my breath. Squeezing and pushing out every bit of goodness and hope and light. I try to suck in oxygen but my lungs don't move. The cramping sensation in my chest gets tighter, until I think I actually may be having a heart attack.

I'm on my hands and knees, with one arm reaching out toward our door.

Correction.

Beck's door.

Not mine anymore.

I wait, and then wait some more for him to open it back up, my chest caving in on itself.

And I wait.

My head drops, hair falling in a curtain as I stare at the dark gray carpeting. My arm succumbs to gravity and my palm presses down for balance. I remember to that moment when I first saw JT on TV and vomited all over my threadbare carpet. Back then, I had been assaulted with terrifying memories that I realized were not just nightmares but waking, living, breathing events that had happened me. I was caught under an avalanche of fear and shame and self-loathing. I vomited and cried and expelled snot all over the carpet.

Not this time.

Right now, my eyes are bone-dry and I know this is because my body is shutting down, refusing to accept the magnitude of what I just lost. If I really consider everything that Beck is to me, and that I will no longer have it again, I'm not sure I'll physically survive it.

I'm sure that if I give credence to the fact that I just destroyed every bit of trust and care he had for me, my heart will end up curling in on itself. It will form into a dried-out, blackened knot of bitterness that I'll never overcome, and it will be far worse than any pain I've experienced in my life.

Yes, even more painful than *that*, and I don't have it in me for that type of suffering again.

So I have to push past . . . ignore . . . obliviate.

Lurching up onto my knees, I place my hands on my thighs for balance, and try once again to catch a breath. Grudgingly, my lungs expand and pull precious life into me and I let it out in a quavering sigh of defeat.

My gaze falls to the floor again, and I see that the contents of my purse have been scattered clear across the hall. I take in another deep breath, feel my heart still cramping in agony.

God, it hurts.

So much.

My heart, my chest, my head.

My lungs.

My bones. I even feel the crushing weight of defeat and loss in my bones.

Reaching out, I grab the strap of my purse and pull it in to me. I look into the gaping opening and see my wallet and key chain still inside. I pull the keys out and work off Beck's condo key. It takes me a moment and I realize I'm clumsily fumbling with it because I feel dizzy.

I consciously pull in another lungful of oxygen, realizing that the pain just on the other side of my breastbone is so all consuming it's taken away my body's natural ability to want to live. To even pull in the basic necessity of the air I need to survive.

Deep breath in.

Let it out.

In.

Out.

Breathe, Sela. Just fucking breathe.

An agonized sob pops out of my mouth as images of Beck's face flash before me. His look so angry and condemning. His unwillingness to give me five precious minutes to explain myself. I jerk the key from the ring and fling it at the door, a sudden burst of anger filling me up and giving me strength.

Just as fast it gushes out of me.

And for a brief, glorious moment, my chest relaxes . . . the cramping fades. I take in a tentative breath and find my lungs expand easily. A swirling sensation of relief, and I use the opportunity to stand.

I keep still, afraid some other nasty or wretched emotion will take me hostage. I wait for it to come, to make my knees buckle, but . . . nothing.

I feel absolutely nothing.

"Beck," I begged with a sob. "JT . . . he raped me."

He hesitated, eyes wide with shock and face draining of blood. I even reached out to him, not once doubting that he'd want to help me.

But then my world crashed again when he looked down upon me with disgust and said, "Yet another lie, Sela," before slamming the door on me.

I think about Beck just moments ago, pushing me out his door, looking at me with disgust and calling me—the rape victim—a liar.

And nothing.

Absolute emptiness within me, but it's actually a blissful feeling, because it doesn't hurt.

My gaze falls back down to the carpet. Lip gloss, loose change, tampons, chewing gum, and a matchbook I took from a jazz club that Beck and I went to. A keepsake, so to speak.

Tiny cramp in my chest. I push it away and face the elevator, ignoring all of the scattered items.

I turn my back and leave it all behind.

All of it.

Behind.

PHOTO: MARIE KILLEN

Since the release of her debut contemporary romance novel, *Off Sides,* in January 2013, SAWYER BENNETT has released more than thirty books and has been featured on both the *USA Today* and *New York Times* bestseller lists on multiple occasions.

A reformed trial lawyer from North Carolina, Sawyer uses real-life experience to create relatable, sexy stories that appeal to a wide array of readers. From new adult to erotic contemporary romance, Sawyer writes something for just about everyone.

Sawyer likes her Bloody Marys strong, her martinis dirty, and her heroes a combination of the two. When not bringing fictional romance to life, Sawyer is a chauffeur, stylist, chef, maid, and personal assistant to a very active toddler, as well as full-time servant to two adorably naughty dogs. She believes in the goodness of others and that a bad day can be cured with a great workout, cake, or a combination of the two.

sawyerbennett.com
Facebook.com/bennettbooks
@bennettbooks

ABOUT THE TYPE

This book was set in Galliard, a typeface designed in 1978 by Matthew Carter (b. 1937) for the Mergenthaler Linotype Company. Galliard is based on the sixteenth-century typefaces of Robert Granjon (1513–89).